◇◇◇

What would it be like, he asked himself,
walking slowly in the direction of his house,
where his wife Anna was waiting for him—
sweet, kind Anna, whom he had ended up
marrying in order to *settle down* (isn't that what
it was called, in times past, in the world of
Parisian courtesans?—*Oh Maati, you and your
French references...* and sometimes she would add:
You aren't even French, you're Moroccan.)
—a world where everything was *foreign*?

◇◇◇

THE
CURIOUS CASE
OF DASSOUKINE'S
TROUSERS

—

Fouad Laroui

TRANSLATED FROM THE FRENCH BY
EMMA RAMADAN

INTRODUCTION BY
LAILA LALAMI

DEEP VELLUM PUBLISHING
DALLAS, TEXAS

Deep Vellum Publishing
3000 Commerce St., Dallas, Texas 75226
deepvellum.org · @deepvellum

Deep Vellum Publishing is a 501C3
nonprofit literary arts organization founded in 2013.

ISBN: 978-1-941920-26-8 (paperback) · 978-1-941920-27-5 (ebook)
LIBRARY OF CONGRESS CONTROL NUMBER: 2015960722
—
Cover design & typesetting by Anna Zylicz · annazylicz.com

Text set in Bembo, a typeface modeled on typefaces cut by Francesco Griffo
for Aldo Manuzio's printing of *De Aetna* in 1495 in Venice.

Distributed by Consortium Book Sales & Distribution.

Printed in the United States of America on acid-free paper.

Table of Contents

—

INTRODUCTION
Laila Lalami

A Saturday morning in Casablanca. Nagib and Hamid sit in a café, bored and about to have a pointless argument about an article from *Le Matin du Sahara*, when their friend Dadine offers to tell them a story instead—the story of Bennani's bodyguard. A bodyguard, they ask in amazement. A bodyguard, here in Casablanca? As Dadine tells it, this Bennani fellow was one of those rich teens from the Lycée Lyautey, and he turned up to a celebration the less fortunate students had organized with a bodyguard in tow.

This was in the old days, Dadine continues, when high school students could still host a dance party in Casablanca without worrying about who might notice their beer, or who might blow themselves up in a crowded street. In the old days, when even the children of the poor could attend an institution like the Lycée Lyautey. "Happy days!" Nagib and Hamid say. "Joyous age!" Yes, Dadine notes wryly, this was in "an age when three people out of two were in the police, where snitches abounded, where you could be denounced by your own shadow—the bitch."

"Bennani's bodyguard" is pure Fouad Laroui. Told mostly in dialogue, with the reader in the position of an eavesdropper, it gives us characters who are caught between rosy nostalgia and dark humor. Laroui's prose moves fluidly between languages, between

3

high and low culture, between affecting personal commentary and sharp cultural observations. This constant code-switching is no doubt a testament to a life lived between cultures, and made all the richer for it.

Laroui was born in the border town of Oujda, in eastern Morocco, in 1958. After completing his high school baccalauréat in Casablanca, he trained at the prestigious École des Ponts et Chaussées in Paris, then returned home to Morocco, where he worked for the Office Chérifien des Phosphates in the small town of Khouribga. But in 1990, he moved to the Netherlands and taught himself Dutch, reportedly by reading the newspaper and watching television. He is currently a professor of French literature at the University of Amsterdam and writes frequently, often in a contrarian tone, on subjects ranging from economics to immigration.

Laroui's first novel, *Les Dents du topographe*, was published in 1996 to wide critical acclaim and helped make his reputation, both in his native Morocco and in France. The narrator of *Les Dents* is a high school student who is arrested as a subversive because he started something called PAP (Parti Anti-Publicité or Anti-Publicity Party), mostly in an effort to rid his town of posters. He is questioned and later released, but he decides to leave Morocco for Europe, where he finishes his studies, then returns, years later, as a college graduate. His old friends, meanwhile, have not fared so well, ending up dead, in jail, or under the power of religious fanaticism.

The political agitator turned disillusioned graduate is a familiar character in post-independence Moroccan fiction (and nowhere is this character more brilliantly realized than in Driss Chraibi's *The Simple Past*), but in the case of Fouad Laroui, the story is told with an eye on the absurd, and laced with caustic humor. *Les Dents du topographe* was followed by some twenty other novels, story collections, and collections of poetry, including, most notably, *Méfiez vous des parachutistes* (1999), *Le Maboul* (2001), *La Fin tragique de Philomène Tralala* (2003), and *Tu n'as rien compris à Hassan II*.

Ten years ago, after lively discussions with Fouad Laroui on religion and secularism in Amsterdam, I tried to interest American editors in his *De l'islamisme. Une réfutation personnelle du totalitarisme religieux (On Islamism: A Personal Refutation of Religious Fundamentalism)*. But all this was to no avail. So you can imagine my delight that Deep Vellum is finally introducing the American public to this original, independent, and multitalented writer.

The Curious Case of Dassoukine's Trousers is a comic book, occasionally even a farce. The title character, for example, is a government official who lands in Belgium with the intent of buying 20 million pounds of wheat (or is it 200 million pounds?) for Morocco, but his trousers—the only pair he has brought on his short trip—are stolen. Now he must show up to his minister's meeting in golf pants purchased at the Oxfam store around the corner. The European delegates greet him with shock and, depending on their country of origin, think of him as a thief, a freeloader, a hoaxer, or a "Moro." But beneath the humor is Laroui's constant concern with power and displacement. His prose is delightfully energetic, filled with double entendres, and he is not afraid to experiment with syntactic structures, as he does in the story "Dislocation."

In its exploration of culture, identity, and religious dogma, *Dassoukine* consistently make us laugh while it makes us think. Laroui turns his appraising gaze on the foibles and foolishness of his characters—with irreverence, but never without tenderness.

Santa Monica, January 2016

THE CURIOUS CASE OF DASSOUKINE'S TROUSERS

"Belgium really is the birthplace of Surrealism," sighs Dassoukine, staring into the distance.

I don't respond because this phrase seems like a prologue—and in the face of a prologue, what can you do but await what follows, resigned. My commensal examines his mug of beer suspiciously, even though we are, after all, in the country that saw the birth of this pretty blonde, sometimes brunette, child—in an abbey, I'm told. The server eyes us. In this superb spot situated on the Grand Place of Brussels, opposite the Maison du Cygne, we form a trio hanging on this thesis: "Belgium really is the birthplace of Surrealism." This incipit is still floating in the air when Dassoukine decides to elaborate.

"What just happened to me, in any case, exceeds all bounds."

I restrain myself from adding: "And when boundaries are crossed…"

He begins:

"So, I set out yesterday from Morocco on a very delicate mission. You know the grain harvest is off to a bad start in our country—it has rained, but not a lot. We are in desperate need of flour, but where to find it? Ukraine is in flames, the Russians cling tightly to their crops, it's a long way to Australia. There's only one solution: Europe. The government sends me to buy flour from Brussels. They've entrusted this mission to me. The country's future is at risk. At the airport, in Rabat, they're all on the tarmac, the ministers standing straight as yews, to bid me *bon voyage* as if their fate depended on little old me. Well, little...I'm taller than all of them by a head. The prime minister shakes my hand while the airplane engines roar and my eyes blur:

"'Get the best price, my boy, the best price! The budget of the state depends on your negotiating skills.'

"He nearly pulled my ear, as if to say, 'the homeland is counting on you, grenadier.' I board the plane and set sail for the haystacks. On the Place Jourdan in Brussels I get a room in the hotel where high-flying diplomats normally stay. Check-in, shower, quick glance at the TV—the world still exists. I'll spare you the details. I go down to have a drink at the bar. Surprise! While I've come to the land of Tintin to buy wheat, suddenly I find myself on the first floor at a soirée whose theme is—adjusting our glasses and leaning in to look at the placard—'the promotion of Alsatian wine and cuisine.' Curious. I had thought the gastronomy on the borders of the Rhine could stand up for itself—didn't the Maginot Line used to be there? But anyway...I mingle among the guests. Everyone seems to be enjoying themselves and no one seems to notice this tall freeloading foreigner who tomorrow will be buying twenty million pounds of wheat. No one...except for two gentlemen."

"Two gentlemen?"

"Yes, one plus one."

"You pronounce the 't' when you say it?"

Dassoukine looks at me, dumbstruck.

"I'm telling you about the fiasco of the century and the only thing you're worried about is whether you say 'two gentlemen' or 'two gennelmen'?"

"Apologies."

"So, two gen-TUHL-men. The first one is a waiter who asks me politely if I might lend him a hand, he has to change a tablecloth, I don't know why. Possessing, like all servers from Brussels, only two arms, he hands me his tray, full of petits fours, for the time it takes him to carry out the operation he's determined to accomplish. It's then that another guy (the second one I mentioned), a tall string bean, clumsy but perfectly well-bred, hits me with his elbow, while I balance the tray on my open palm, as if I had never done anything else in my life—me, the grandson of a kaid and the son of a prime minister."

"No one's denying that."

"Except for the second guy, who, after apologizing for having (nearly) knocked over my tray—why am I saying 'my' tray, it's mad how we adapt to degradation—babbling in multilingual apologies—I detect some Hungarian in his English accent and some Latvian in his fumbled French; so, after babbling a number of apologies as if he had surprised Sissi naked in a back alley, what does he do?"

"What does he do?"

"Well, he picks up a mini-toast from my tray and thanks me while bowing slightly."

"Indeed a polite man, then, albeit Hungarian."

"That's not the problem, idiot! He thanked me *as if I were a waiter*."

"There are no dishonorable jobs."

"In the absolute sense, no. Perhaps. But come on, I'm in Brussels to buy two hundred million pounds of wheat!"

"Inflation."

"Around ten o'clock, after savoring the dishes prepared by some of the best chefs—might as well—and after wearing out my tongue appreciating wines that I didn't even know existed, I decide to go back to my room. Brussels is going through a heat wave: it's still 102 degrees outside. Unable to sleep in such heat, I read the *Mémoires* of the Belgian king. And because I'm not crazy about air conditioning, I turn it off, like the peasant I am, opting to open the big window instead. My room is on the second floor…"

"Do I need every detail?"

"…but here the floors are high, so it was really the third floor. Just after midnight, I turn out the lights and contemplate wheat and wheat farms. That's me: professional down to the muslin. Not long after, half asleep, I hear the window bang and the curtains move, like in those horror movies that that can't even scare a cat. I say to myself that the long-awaited storm has finally arrived— *Levez-vous vite, orages désirés…*—and that the atmosphere will cool down. I nestle into my bed and dream of haystacks. A few minutes later, I'm woken up again, this time by the sounds of metal. Clang! Clang! What's going on now? I open my eyes and, stupefied, I see a hand hanging from the window railing! I sit up bellowing (*What is that racket?*) and jump out of bed. The hand disappears. This is bad. Should I lean out the window and risk finding myself face to face with Dracula or Peter Lorre? I'm brave—you know me—but I have my limits. So I call reception. The operator picks up right away—we are, after all, in a nice hotel—I inform him in two words of the incident, he asks me if it's room service that I'm trying to reach, I add some details, he tells me that, yes, they have fries, I tell him about the wandering hand, he replies mayonnaise, I start over, enunciating my words; after a stunned silence, the man gets a hold of himself and tells me he'll call the police right away.

"After replacing the receiver, I go to look out the window anyway, armed with the *Financial Times* rolled up into a bat, in case the salmon color should frighten away the zombies. I see nothing, no one in this serene, Belgian night. My room looks out onto the Etterbeek, there are some bushes, but I search far and wide; the cat burglar has disappeared. Roughly speaking, there's a good thirty feet between my bedroom window and the ground. The wall is made of brick, there's no gutter, nothing for a person to hang on to. There's a little ledge under my window, but it's narrow. And even then you still have to get there, and somehow stay there."

"Thorough report."

"The police arrive rapidly and get to work. There are four of them, debonair but industrious. They survey the surroundings of the hotel with flashlights, they smoke out some cats, drive out three spiders, cry out in *bruxellois*, but they don't find anything human. They leave, taking down my statement. According to them, it must have been like in a circus act: three or four men climb on one another's shoulders, the one on top reaches the window, enters the room, and grabs any objects of value. Then they disappear into the neighboring thickets—beautiful thickets, by the way, I recommend them, look up the Parc Léopold. I think to myself that I dodged a bullet, given that my laptop was on the shelf right by the window. All the secrets of the Kingdom—ours, not Belgium's—will remain secret. I go back to sleep, pretty perplexed."

"And the metal noises?"

"Forgotten! I had more important things to do than wonder about the whisper of the world. The next morning: toilet, shower, shave, after-shave—the ritual of a minister on a mission. I start to get dressed and then, stupor and shudders, as a local author once said: no more trousers! *Nada, niente!* I had left them folded, flat on the suitcase, close to the window. And at that hour, they were conspicuously absent! In a flash, I understand everything: the thief had taken my trousers, in which I had left a pile of change. And it was these coins, falling out of the pockets, that had woken me up!"

"Voilà, mystery solved."

"One hell of a lucky break, I said to myself *in petto*. Normally, I empty the pockets of my trousers before folding them at night. But that night, for whatever reason, I hadn't. The noise woke me up and the thief left without my computer, which holds the plans for the nuclear missiles stashed under the Place Jemaa el Fna in Marrakech. However, I had also left some bills in the pockets, and so I'm out 320 euros. Bah, money isn't everything... The problem—or should I say the *tragedy*?... the catastrophe?—is that I don't have any other trousers. For the two-day trip, I had brought only the *saroual* I was wearing. Why complicate things? Two shirts, yes, but only one pair of pants: I'm not Patino the Tin King, or an English lord. So, *nix* pairs of trousers and Europe awaits me at nine o'clock sharp. I go down to the reception in my pajamas. The manager is there, impeccably dressed. He is already up-to-date on my misadventure. Alas, he tells me, all the stores are still

FOUAD LAROUI

closed at this morning hour. Brow furrowed, he thinks through a few different possibilities. He could go to his house and bring me one of his pairs of trousers, or he could ask the employees, but these suggestions, born of Belgian goodwill, come crashing down when faced with this irrefutable reality: I am taller than all these Samaritans. I would look like a half-drowned Nixon! Standing in the hotel lobby, we look at each other, sheepish, and the seconds pass.

"'I hardly dare suggest it to you…' he says to me while adjusting his glasses with an extremely distinguished air.

"'Go on, go on! Anything would be better than being stark naked or wearing a barrel around my waist!'

"'Two minutes from here, at the corner of rue de l'Étang, there's an Oxfam Solidarité shop that sells used clothing.'

"'But it'll be closed!'

"'My aunt is the manager, call her, she'll open the shop. She lives right around the corner.'"

Dassoukine swallows a mouthful of coffee and assumes a tragic air.

"He who has never crossed the Place Jourdan in his pajamas, hair disheveled, searching for an act of charity even though he is the grandson of a kaid, has no concept of the absurd. I rush into the shop where an old woman is waiting for me with an angelic smile.

"'My God, you're a giant,' she chirps, panicked.

"'At your service, madame.'

"'The only thing we have in your size is this.'

"She unhooks a rag and hands it to me. Prepare the funeral

13

arrangements! They're golf trousers, the work of a mad tailor, the trappings of a clown. Oh they have lived, possibly several lives, and hard ones at that. The original colors are now faded but it's obvious they must have clashed violently in the old days. You can see beneath the fabric, beneath the canvas, I should say, a yellow, a yucky brown, an evanescent green, a burnt amber, red diamonds layered on top…but we mustn't entirely write off the wreckage, because there is one undeniable advantage: they are exactly my size. I throw five euros on the counter, I forget my pajamas and rush toward the assembly hall: it's right around the corner, at the end of rue Froissart. The orderly raises an eyebrow when he notices my trousers but my papers are in order and he grants me entry while deploring in a low voice the end of European civilization. I enter the hall, where my interruption causes a sensation. The members of the committee, who are already there, on a sort of platform, gawk at me with bulging eyes, looking only below the belt, as if I had been reduced to two legs."

"We are but ants in the grand scheme of things."

"I sit down on a chair opposite these *messieurs-dames* of Europe and I prepare to present my plea. I fix my gaze on the eyes of the committee…and then I nearly fall out of my chair. For who is presiding over the committee? I'll give you three guesses."

"Uhh…"

"The Hungarian!"

"Attila the Hun?"

"No, moron! The Hungarian from the day before, civilized to the core, the grandson of the Archduke and the Bourbons. He looks at me, knitting his brow ('I know that face…'), then his mouth gapes open ('No, not him, not the waiter from yesterday!'), and then I have before me the personification of Hungarian stupefaction and commiseration ('It's really him!'), and then he leans toward his colleagues, distraught, and starts speaking to them in a low voice. He forgets to turn off his microphone; the interpreter, imperturbable, thus continues to translate—it is his job after all—and so I intrude on this discussion centered on me, and in particular on my trousers. Monsieur *Hongre* recounts the reception from the night before and tells them I was the waiter and that, with great dexterity, I walked around with a tray filled with petits fours and incidentally almost poured them onto him; but, he adds with a sense of fairness through which I recognize the true son of a *grande tente* family (even if they are Habsburgs), that I deserve credit for serving them with great professionalism. The Archduke's report flabbergasts his peers. Then Europe, as always, divides itself. The Slovak reckons I was making off with the leftovers from the buffet because I didn't have any money, but the Englishman retorts that I came here on a plane and not a flying carpet, and therefore I must have some means, I couldn't be completely 'skint.' The Italian taps his chin, suspecting some *combinazione*, but what? The Spaniard grumbles something about the 'Moros' who never learn. Was I perhaps staging a hoax, for whatever obscure reason? The Frenchman, Cartesian to his eyebrows, expresses his doubts: being very familiar with Morocco, he can't imagine a minister of His Majesty arriving dirt poor (much like the wheat) in Brussels; what if he was a doppelgänger?

"'Doppelgänger?' interrupts the German. *Ach so…*But which one? Yesterday's *Kellner* or this guy, here, on the stand?'

"The committee, as one single man, straightens up and examines me with a suspicious air. Am I really myself? Or a clown imposter? Or a lackey with a big head?

"The Englishman clears his throat and then squeals in my direction:

"'*Exckiousez-moi*…This is highly unusual but…*Pievons-nous vouâr vos…papiers* d'identity?'

"It's an international incident. I straighten up, tall in my multicolored breeches, and I play out a great scene of Third World indignation in the face of Western arrogance. What is this, huh? I must be dreaming! Would you demand to see the papers of an American or Russian minister? Or even Albanian? Shall I, while we're at it, produce my anthropometric measurements? My criminal record? My vaccinations for dengue fever and cholera? The Hungarian, miming gestures of appeasement, motions for me to sit back down, and snubs perfidious Albion, now muttering threats.

"I go back to my discourse on wheat, 'which we formerly exported to the Roman Empire,' but no one is listening to me, no one cares about the Rome of antiquity. Then the Hungarian makes an imperial gesture and adjourns the session. These *messieurs-dames* are going to make a decision. They ask me to wait in an adjoining room, where they serve me coffee and chocolate—go on, have a bite, it's Belgian. Half an hour later, an usher comes to fetch me: the committee has come to a decision."

"Well?"

"Well, I got the flour for nothing. They remembered, quite pertinently, that there was an emergency stock for desperate cases, like for Somalia, Chad, and other countries where the ministers dress in rags. Pounds of grain for free! Tonight they're throwing me an extravagant reception at the Rabat airport. 'The man who saved his country a hundred thousand euros!' It's really my trousers they should be honoring."

He looks outside, pensively. The façades of the Grand Place glisten. Dassoukine sighs.

"The most beautiful place in the world, they say. And they're right. But I remember only the Place Jourdan, where I found myself dressed as a clown and a servant in order to better serve my country. Who will ever believe that?"

DISLOCATION

What would it be like, he asked himself, a world where everything was *foreign?*

What would it be like, he asked himself, walking slowly in the direction of his house, a world where everything was *foreign?*

What would it be like, he asked himself, walking slowly in the direction of his house, where his wife Anna was waiting for him, a world where everything was *foreign?*

What would it be like, he asked himself, walking slowly in the direction of his house, where his wife Anna was waiting for him—sweet, kind Anna—a world where everything was *foreign?*

What would it be like, he asked himself, walking slowly in the direction of his house, where his wife Anna was waiting for him—sweet, kind Anna, whom he had ended up marrying in order to *settle down* (isn't that what it was called, in times past, in the world of Parisian courtesans?)—a world where everything was *foreign?*

What would it be like, he asked himself, walking slowly in the

direction of his house, where his wife Anna was waiting for him—
sweet, kind Anna, whom he had ended up marrying in order to
settle down (isn't that what it was called, in times past, in the world
of Parisian courtesans?—*Oh Maati, you and your French references…*)—a world where everything was *foreign?*

What would it be like, he asked himself, walking slowly in the
direction of his house, where his wife Anna was waiting for him—
sweet, kind Anna, whom he had ended up marrying in order to
settle down (isn't that what it was called, in times past, in the world
of Parisian courtesans?—*Oh Maati, you and your French references…*
and sometimes she would add: *You aren't even French, you're Moroccan.*)—a world where everything was *foreign?*

What would it be like, he asked himself, walking slowly in the
direction of his house, where his wife Anna was waiting for him—
sweet, kind Anna, whom he had ended up marrying in order to
settle down (isn't that what it was called, in times past, in the world
of Parisian courtesans?—*Oh Maati, you and your French references…*
and sometimes she would add: *You aren't even French, you're Moroccan.* He had tried one day to explain to her that he was Moroccan
by birth, in body, but "French in the head."…She had laughed
in his face, and even he wasn't very convinced by his *pro domo*
plea)—a world where everything was *foreign?*

What would it be like, he asked himself, walking slowly in the
direction of his house, where his wife Anna was waiting for him—
sweet, kind Anna, whom he had ended up marrying in order to

settle down (isn't that what it was called, in times past, in the world of Parisian courtesans?—*Oh Maati, you and your French references…* and sometimes she would add: "*You aren't even French, you're Moroccan.*" He had tried one day to explain to her that he was Moroccan by birth, in body, but "French in the head."…She had laughed in his face, and even he wasn't very convinced by his *pro domo* plea. But here, for God's sake! Here, in Utrecht, wasn't he ten times more of a foreigner than he would have been if he had moved to Nantes or Montpellier?)—a world where everything was *foreign?*

What would it be like, he asked himself, walking slowly in the direction of his house, where his wife Anna was waiting for him— sweet, kind Anna, whom he had ended up marrying in order to *settle down* (isn't that what it was called, in times past, in the world of Parisian courtesans?—*Oh Maati, you and your French references…* and sometimes she would add: *You aren't even French, you're Moroccan.* He had tried one day to explain to her that he was Moroccan by birth, in body, but "French in the head."…She had laughed in his face, and even he wasn't very convinced by his *pro domo* plea. But here, for God's sake! Here, in Utrecht, wasn't he ten times more of a foreigner than he would have been if he had moved to Nantes or Montpellier? Over there, the trees would have had familiar names, the trees and the animals and the household items at the supermarket; over there he wouldn't have needed to consult a dictionary to buy a mop)—a world where everything was *foreign?*

What would it be like, he asked himself, walking slowly in the direction of his house, where his wife Anna was waiting for him—sweet, kind Anna, whom he had ended up marrying in order to *settle down* (isn't that what it was called, in times past, in the world of Parisian courtesans?—*Oh Maati, you and your French references*…and sometimes she would add: *You aren't even French, you're Moroccan.* He had tried one day to explain to her that he was Moroccan by birth, in body, but "French in the head."…She had laughed in his face, and even he wasn't very convinced by his *pro domo* plea. But here, for God's sake! Here, in Utrecht, wasn't he ten times more of a foreigner than he would have been if he had moved to Nantes or Montpellier? Over there, the trees would have had familiar names, the trees and the animals and the household items at the supermarket; over there, he wouldn't have needed to consult a dictionary to buy a mop—a *mop*, goddamnit! It had come to this, he who had dreamed of "changing the world"— what was it again, that Marx quotation he had repeated with elation, with a sort of pride by anticipation—like a program, like a project…ah yes: "Philosophers have only interpreted the world; the point is to change it!" He added long ago, a bit of a pedant, but a winning pedant: "the eleventh thesis on Feuerbach," yes, yes: "the point is to *change* it!")—a world where everything was *foreign?*

What would it be like, he asked himself, walking slowly in the direction of his house, where his wife Anna was waiting for him— sweet, kind Anna, whom he had ended up marrying in order to *settle down* (isn't that what it was called, in times past, in the world of Parisian courtesans?—*Oh Maati, you and your French references*… and sometimes she would add: *You aren't even French, you're Moroccan.* He had tried one day to explain to her that he was Moroccan by birth, in body, but "French in the head."…She had laughed in his face, and even he wasn't very convinced by his *pro domo* plea. But here, for God's sake! Here, in Utrecht, wasn't he ten times more of a foreigner than he would have been if he had moved to Nantes or Montpellier? Over there, the trees would have had familiar names, the trees and the animals and the household items at the supermarket; over there, he wouldn't have needed to consult a dictionary to buy a mop—a *mop*, goddamnit! It had come to this, he who had dreamed of "changing the world"—what was it again, that Marx quotation he had repeated with elation, with a sort of pride by anticipation—like a program, like a project…ah yes: "Philosophers have only interpreted the world; the point is to change it!" He added long ago, a bit of a pedant, but a winning pedant: "the eleventh thesis on Feuerbach," yes, yes: "the point is to *change* it!" But today? Life's vicissitudes…Here he is, an immigrant in a world where he doesn't know the codes, or only very vaguely, a world where each day he must discover the codes—a discreet nudge from Anna, the nudge in his side that night when he had enthusiastically plunged his spoon into the soup bowl, the night when her parents were visiting—hey, we have to wait for the short prayer giving thanks to God for the food on the table—wasn't her father a pastor of the Reformed Church of the Netherlands?)—a world where everything was *foreign?*

What would it be like, he asked himself, walking slowly—more and more slowly, as if he wasn't in any hurry to arrive—in the direction of his house, where his wife Anna was waiting for him— sweet, kind Anna—but sweet and kind because he never annoyed her, having decided once and for all that he would move to the Netherlands, that they had accepted him, and that it was out of the question, consequently, to import anything of his own customs, habits, behaviors from his native Morocco into this country where he was rebuilding his life, no: where he was continuing his life— Anna, whom he had ended up marrying in order to *settle down* (isn't that what it was called, in times past, in the world of Parisian courtesans? (Doesn't Proust use that expression somewhere?)—*Oh Maati, you and your French references…*and sometimes she would add: *You aren't even French, you're Moroccan.* (It wasn't mean, just a bit teasing—Anna didn't establish any hierarchy between Moroccans and the French—which stunned him, and for which he was extremely grateful to her.) He had tried one day to explain to her that he was Moroccan by birth, in body, but "French in the head."…(Suddenly he remembered the title of the novel-essay by Günter Grass, *Headbirths or, the Germans are Dying Out.*) She had laughed in his face, and even he wasn't very convinced by his *pro domo* plea. (He got angry when Anna contradicted him, and even more so when he knew that she was right, at least partially—but he never let it show, true to his credo: "I am not at home here, I am a sort of guest in this country.") But here, for God's sake! Here, in Utrecht, wasn't he ten times more of a foreigner than he would have been if he had moved to Nantes or Montpellier? Over there, the trees would have had familiar names, the trees and the animals and the household items at the supermarket; over there, he wouldn't have needed to consult a dictionary to buy a mop—a *mop*, goddamnit! It had come to this, he who had dreamed of "changing the world"—what was it again, that Marx quotation he had repeated with elation (in his youth, for now opportunities for citing Marx were rare…), with a sort of pride by anticipation—like a program, like a project…ah yes: "Philosophers have only interpreted the world; the point is to change it!" He added long ago, a bit of a pedant, but a winning pedant: "the eleventh thesis on Feuerbach," yes, yes: "the point is to *change* it!" But today? Life's vicissitudes…Here he is, an immigrant in a world where he doesn't know the codes, or only very vaguely, a world where each day he must discover the codes—a discreet nudge from Anna, the nudge in his side that night when he had enthusiastically plunged his spoon into the soup bowl, the night when her parents were visiting—hey, we have to wait for the short prayer giving thanks to God for the food on the table—wasn't her father a pastor of the Reformed Church of the Netherlands? Hastily putting the spoon back down next to the bowl, he had clasped his hands with unction and lowered his head—they didn't expect him to do the short prayer (what was it called? "Doing grace"?) but at least he had given the impression of reflecting with them, so that he would be slightly of their world)—a world where everything was *foreign?*

What would it be like… he asked himself, walking slowly—more and more slowly, as if he wasn't in any hurry to arrive—in the direction of his house (*their* house), where his wife Anna was waiting for him—sweet, kind Anna—but sweet and kind because he never annoyed her, having decided once and for all that he would move to the Netherlands, that they had accepted him (they had even given him a passport), and that it was out of the question, consequently, to import anything of his own customs, habits, behaviors from his native Morocco into this country where he was rebuilding his life—no: where he was continuing his life— Anna whom he had ended up marrying in order to *settle down* (isn't that what it was called, in times past, in the world of Parisian courtesans? (Doesn't Proust use this expression somewhere? Concerning Odette, perhaps?)—*Oh Maati, you and your French references*...and sometimes she would add, with a smile: *You aren't even French, you're Moroccan!* (It wasn't mean, just a bit teasing— Anna didn't establish any hierarchy between Moroccans and the French—which stunned him, and for which he was extremely grateful to her—it was so new, a country where he was just as well regarded, or just as poorly regarded [depending on the person], as the French. At least there's that in exile.) He had tried one day to explain to her that he was Moroccan by birth, in body, but "French in the head."...(Suddenly he remembered the title of the novel-essay by Günter Grass, *Headbirths or, the Germans are Dying Out.* Today he could read it in German: *Kopfgeburten oder die Deutschen sterben aus.* While learning Dutch, he had incidentally also learned German. At least there's that in exile (*bis*). I'm cold, he said to himself sometimes with bitter irony, I'm cold and I eat tasteless things, but at least I've learned German, the language of the philosophers, and now I know the exact meaning of *aufheben*. We were so impressed by them, the Althussers and the consorts, the Derridas, the Glucksmanns, in Paris, when they threw out words like that one, without translating them, as if they were using an abracadabra that only they could access.) She had laughed in his face, and even he wasn't very convinced by his *pro domo* plea.

(He got angry when Anna contradicted him, and even more so when he knew that she was right, at least partially—but he never let it show, true to his credo:"I am not at home here, I am a sort of guest in this country.") But here, for God's sake! Here, in Utrecht, wasn't he ten times more of a foreigner than he would have been if he had moved to Nantes or Montpellier? Over there, the trees would have had familiar names, the trees and the animals and the household items at the supermarket; over there, he wouldn't have needed to consult a dictionary to buy a mop—a *mop*, goddamnit! It had come to this, he who had dreamed of "changing the world"—what was it again, that Marx quotation he had repeated with elation (in his youth, for now opportunities for citing Marx were rare—at university he had seen people defend a thesis in economics, in sociology, without being able to define *surplus value* or *the tendency of the rate of profit to fall*), a sort of pride by anticipation—like a program, like a project…ah yes: "Philosophers have only interpreted the world; the point is to change it!" He added long ago, a bit of a pedant, but a winning pedant: "the eleventh thesis on Feuerbach," yes, yes:"the point is to *change* it!" But today? Life's vicissitudes…Here he is, an immigrant in a world where he doesn't know the codes, or only very vaguely, a world where each day he must discover the codes—a discreet nudge from Anna, the nudge in his side that night when he had enthusiastically plunged his spoon into the soup bowl, the night when her parents were visiting—hey, we have to wait for the short prayer giving thanks to God for the food on the table—wasn't her father a pastor of the Reformed Church of the Netherlands? Hadn't he accepted, this strict father (but not overly), bearded like Jehovah (but not overly), Bach amateur (without moderation), that his daughter marry a foreigner? Shouldn't he be grateful to him? Even if it was possible to read this entire story differently, and view him, the foreigner, as the loser in the affair; to paint a picture, passing from one German to another, from Marx to Nietzsche: "This one went forth in quest of truth as a hero, and at last got for himself a small decked-up lie: his marriage he calleth it." A dressed-up lie (so sweet, so kind) that nudged him in the ribs…Hastily putting the spoon back down next to the bowl, he had clasped his hands (he who had never done so in his country, who had never prayed, nor even entered a mosque) and lowered his head—they didn't expect him to do the short prayer (what was it called? "Doing grace?") but at least he had given the impression of reflecting with them, so that he would be slightly of their world—a world where everything was *foreign?*

What would it be like, he asked himself, walking slowly…

…*more and more slowly; he ended up stopping right at the corner of Transvaalstraat…*

…as if he weren't in any hurry to arrive—in the direction of his house (*their* house)…

…*what is a house? "House" or "home"? Just a cube, a big cube, a cut-out space that the Land Registry had given to him…He watched television there, slept there, watched out of the corner of his eye a beautiful young blonde woman sitting on the sofa, next to him, sometimes forgetting who she was…*

…ah yes, it's my wife…(my wife? What does the possessive sig-nify? What, exactly, do I possess? Am I not rather the thing that is possessed, the domesticated animal—there must be a tiger or a lion at the zoo in Amsterdam who believes he possesses some-thing, who thinks he's wandering around in his home and that the little piece of wood in the form of a tree is his own, beware of the one who comes to rub himself there—it's the conspiracy of the Tall-Blonde-Bach-amateurs that possesses me in the most subtle of manners—I am in their trap—their chains—so be it, I will end up in the cellar, in the hold of a ship beaten by the waves, heading toward the plantation, the zoo…)

…where his wife Anna was waiting—sweet, kind Anna—but sweet and kind because he never annoyed her…

…he had become someone who gives up, a sâdhu*… "Are you two sure you're married? (It was their neighbor who had said this, loquacious, knowing…) You never fight." Exactly, he could have responded: I have renounced—in a world of discord—I have abstracted myself from the world, I am an* abstraction*—indeed, they talk about me that way. Maati? What a curious name…What are you? (*What.*) Ah, Moroccan…then comes the succession of adjectives, the abstraction clarifies: Muslim, probably macho, lover of complicated things, tom-tom, and isn't there a big desert in* your country? *(In my country? I live on Transvaalstraat, in Utrecht.) No, I mean: in* your country.

…having decided once and for all that he would move to the Netherlands, that they had accepted him (they had even given him a passport)…

Who had given him a passport? The State, "the coldest of the cold monsters"…Not the neighbor: she probably would have hesitated. You, my compatriot? But do you have, as I do, thirty lifeless bodies in a vault? They are my ancestors, lying down, stiff, they stand guard, in a perpetual procession, where the squirrels run. I go there to decorate their tombs with flowers, you seem to me more like someone who comes to spit on the graves—I have never seen people like you on All Saints' Day, at the cemetery with its pleasant alignment of marble statues…

…and that it was out of the question, consequently, to import anything of his own customs, habits, behaviors from his native Morocco…

…*what did he know of them, anyway?*

…into this country where he was rebuilding his life—no: where he was continuing his life—Anna whom he had ended up marrying in order to *settle down* (isn't that what it was called, in times past, in the world of Parisian courtesans? (Doesn't Proust use this expression somewhere? Concerning Odette, perhaps?)…

…*it had been years since he had last read Proust. He no longer had the opportunity to use him. Or to share him. Simenon, sometimes, not even…*

the newspaper…the sports pages…the television…

—*Oh Maati, you and your French references*…and sometimes she would add, with a smile: *You aren't even French, you're Moroccan!*

That sounds like a reproach. At the corner of Transvaalstraat, where a hundred absolutely identical houses trace converging lines toward the void, everything seems like an accusation that the court clerk, one foresees, will end up summarizing with the following question asked in a glacial tone: "What are you doing here?"

(It wasn't mean, just a bit teasing—Anna didn't establish any hierarchy between Moroccans and the French…)

…nor between the Chinese and the Peruvians, nor between anyone and anybody, like a good little Protestant…

…which stunned him, and for which he was extremely grateful to her—

…up until this instant, this dislocation, Transvaalstraat; he didn't recognize gratitude for anything anymore, he didn't recognize anything anymore; he would have preferred that she treat him like a Chinese person rather than say to him: "You are other, but that's okay, we forgive you, and you're equal to all the others"—just as at the zoo, the tiger seems to be the equal of the porcupine, they are fed in the same way, they are loved the same and the placard in front of the enclosure, which designates them very scientifically, which situates them (there is a map of the world and

a red spot to mark the territory where they toil away), so, what about the placard? It's the same for all: tiger, porcupine, or bonobo—but Anna, you're outside of the enclosure, it's your father, younger, beard less white, who points at the bonobo and reads aloud for you the description provided on the placard…

… it was so new, a country where he was just as well regarded, or just as poorly regarded [depending on the person], as the French. At least there's that in exile.) He had tried one day to explain to her that he was Moroccan by birth, in body, but "French in the head."…

…what does that mean, exactly? It's absurd…it's tiresome…my God, everything is escaping me…It's my mind, fittingly, that's liquefy-ing—"France, your coffee is escaping!"—and what will remain, what remains of our loves, if our mind goes to the dogs, nothing but a body, a big sick body, on its back, bigger dead than alive…

(Suddenly he remembered the title of the novel-essay by Günter Grass, *Headbirths or, the Germans are Dying Out*. Today he could read it in German: *Kopfgeburten oder die Deutschen sterben aus…*

…a lot of good it does you! A lot of good it does me! Who is speaking? Who is shouting at me? Who are these snakes…

While learning Dutch, he had incidentally also learned German. At least there's that, in exile (*bis*). I'm cold, he said to himself sometimes with bitter irony, I'm cold and I eat tasteless things, but at least I've learned German, the language of the philosophers, and now I know the exact meaning of *aufheben*. We were really impressed by them, the Althussers and the consorts, the Derridas, the Glucksmanns, in Paris, when they threw out words like that one, without translating them, as if they were using an abracadabra only they could access.)

If they were here, on this street, I would throw a big stone at their heads, a rock I would first need to lift up, aufheben—*but then who, but then what is it in me that enjoys making such bad bilingual puns? Who-then-what-then forces my mouth into a sneer—come on, it's not that funny! —when I'm in the middle of dislocating myself, on the corner of this street…*

She had laughed in his face, and even he wasn't very convinced by his *pro domo* plea. (He got angry when Anna contradicted him, and even more so when he knew that she was right, at least partially—but he never let it show, true to his credo: "I am not at home here, I am a sort of guest in this country.")

…as if one were never at home… a little speck of dust in an unlimited universe. The eternal silence of these infinite spaces frightens me… Or is it "the infinite silence of these eternal spaces frightens me"? And if some people believe they are at home, in this tiny particle of dust, in a tiny corner of a speck, and others are invited here…

But here, for God's sake! Here, in Utrecht, wasn't he ten times more of a foreigner than he would have been if he had moved to Nantes or Montpellier? Over there, the trees would have had familiar names, the trees and the animals and the household items at the supermarket; over there, he wouldn't have needed to consult a dictionary to buy a mop—a *mop*, goddamnit! It had come to this, he who had dreamed of "changing the world"—what was it again, that Marx quotation he had repeated with elation (in his youth, for now opportunities for citing Marx were rare—at university, he had seen people defend a thesis in economics, in sociology, without being able to define *surplus value* or *the tendency of the rate of profit to fall)*...

...but s...! All that's finished, it's history...What use is it to you now, here? All of Marx in the Pléaide...One day, someone will throw it in a dumpster, not understanding anything ("It's French")...Very distinctly, he sees the scene and is submerged in a wave of infinite sadness.Young men, grinning, talking about soccer, throwing his Pléaides one by one into a dumpster full of trash and these millions of words, these millions of dead birds, will rot in a corner of polder.

... with a sort of pride by anticipation—like a program, like a project...ah yes: "Philosophers have only interpreted the world; the point is to change it!"

He mutters, tears in his eyes: Die Philosophen haben die Welt nur verschieden interpretiert; es kömmt drauf an, sie zu verändern. *It finishes as a sob:* verändern! *Take note,* Deus absconditus: *one winter night,Transvaalstraat, in a little town in Holland, a Moroccan in complete dislocation, quoted out loud, in German, the eleventh thesis on Feuerbach. Not a blade of grass trembled,* not a mouse stirred. *(When an oak tree falls in the middle of the forest, does it make a sound? He finally has the answer, but it's too late.)*

He added long ago, a bit of a pedant, but a winning pedant: "the eleventh thesis on Feuerbach," yes, yes: "the point is to *change* it!" But today? Life's vicissitudes…

Let's accuse life, it won't defend itself. Life's a bitch, but at least it shuts up. (Oh…but you're not really going to reproach sweet, kind Anna for her babbling—isn't that what you used to find the most charming about her— that incessant chirping—when she had nothing to say, she hummed…Yes, what charms in the first days, the first months, can perfectly well become a reason to murder ten years later…)

Here he is, an immigrant in a world where he doesn't know the codes, or only very vaguely, a world where each day he must discover the codes—a discreet nudge from Anna, the nudge in his side…

He touches his side, there, on Transvaalstraat, as if feeling the blow again, several months after the incident. To the eyes of the world still intact / It feels grow and weep, unspoken, / Its sharp, underlying crack / Do not touch, it is broken.

…that night when he had enthusiastically plunged his spoon into the soup bowl, the night when her parents were visiting—hey, we have to wait for the short prayer giving thanks to God for the food on the table—wasn't her father a pastor of the Reformed Church of the Netherlands? Hadn't he accepted, this strict father (but not overly), bearded like Jehovah (but not overly), Bach amateur (without moderation)...

All along that horizon line toward the void, at that exact instant, perhaps in one or the other of these absolutely identical houses, a Bach cantata plays...It was here, in this country, in this city, that he discovered the Great Consolation—if he could emerge from this dislocation, start back on his route, drag himself to the living room and slide the Passion *into the CD player...But what kind of passion? ("Here we go, he thinks he's Jesus." And again this phrase steeped in irony clearly formed in his head, boiling over. But who is speaking, after all? He turns around brusquely—but no, he's alone in the embalmed twilight.) Continuing on. "Passion." Wasn't he the one suffering from the great translation that brought him to these shores? Wasn't he persevering in this irrational disorder? Why does man distance himself from his home? Why does he make himself into a* foreigner?

...that his daughter marry a foreigner?

And isn't she a foreigner, too? Vis-à-vis the rest of the world? The vast *world? The infinite spaces?*

Shouldn't he be grateful to him? Even if it was possible to read this entire story differently, and view him, the foreigner, as the loser in the affair; and paint a picture, passing from one German to another, from Marx to Nietzsche:

Didn't he, one day in Turin, disintegrate, as I here decompose? He col-
lapses...he passes a carriage whose coach driver is whipping the horse
violently...wrings his neck and bursts into tears...Nothing here on
Transvaalstraat betrays an animal presence—except for me—tiger, por-
cupine, bonobo—who becomes an animal again as soon as everything
loses its meaning—perhaps a cat will appear—cats, the other conso-
lation—and I would take it under my wing, the wing of the animal
that I am, I would forbid anyone from approaching it...Yes, I would
be rather insane to cry with an animal next to me. My fellow creature,
my brother.

"This one went forth in quest of truth as a hero, and at last got
for himself a small decked-up lie: his marriage he calleth it." A
decked-up lie (so sweet, so kind) that nudged him in the ribs...
Hastily putting the spoon back down next to the bowl, he had
clasped his hands (he who had never done so in his country, who
had never prayed, nor even entered a mosque)...

...too late now: The die is cast. *He wouldn't enter anything anymore.*
Enter here, with your cortege of métèques, *the workforce of immigrants...*
Listen, I am an immigrant. A good war, a good Occupation, and I could
choose ignominy, or indifference, or heroism—and I would end up on a
red poster, and I would scare passersby with how difficult it is to pronounce
my name...

...and lowered his head—they didn't expect him to do the short
prayer (what was it called? "Doing grace?") but at least he had
given the impression of reflecting with them, so that he would be

slightly of their world)—a world where everything was *foreign?*

He leaned his entire body against a tree whose name he probably didn't know—but do trees have names? He closed his eyes. His shirt stuck to his body, he was bathed in a cold sweat that made him shiver. He closed his eyes and saw the unwinding of the rest of Time, without him, without the man who had abstracted himself from a world where everything had become foreign. He saw an excerpt from the next day's paper, a few lines delivering the news about him: *Tragedy on Transvaalstraat. Maati S. hung himself last night. Wife in tears, neighbors in shock ("such a quiet, courteous man, etc.").*

No. In the ferocious struggle against the world, never take the side of the world. He took out a tissue from his pocket and wiped his face. Then he picked up his book bag and slowly turned to face the day...to find himself on the exact street where he had lived for years now, with his wife Anna. *I am Maati S., engineer, employee of City Hall in Utrecht, rank 11, full time, thirty-eight hours per week. I have just experienced a feeling that drowns me, regularly, at a fixed date. (Maybe it has something to do with the moon.) I call it, lacking a better name, "dislocation." How can I explain it... The falcon remains deaf, we don't know why, to the calls of the falconer. It turns and turns and turns in a delirious sky that exacerbates its gyrating. A thousand images of me multiply my terror. Welts, epiphanies, tongues on fire...Everything collapses, there is no more center, in the middle of a night suddenly fallen. There is no more reason. There is no more anything. Who is speaking about what? Who is speaking? Nothing. Nothing. Then, it's incomprehensible, it's a sort of new dawn, it's a small note of the clarinet in the distance, a drum roll, heavy, heady, and the dislocation fades away. These few noises foreshadow a gesture that my wife will make, in a moment, a gesture so banal but containing all the importance I wouldn't be able to give to the world. It's curious, the world coagulates, I come up to the surface. I can even start to walk again. It's enough to put one foot in front of the other.* Let's go! To his great surprise, his left leg obeys. It's an exhausted automaton that walks, book bag in hand, in the direction of his house. It's a trembling hand that rises toward the doorbell, a hesitant finger that grazes it. Sounds of footsteps... Who's there? Is it you, Anna?

"My poor Maati, you look exhausted."

Here he is seated on the sofa (collapsed, rather). He doesn't know how he wound up there, he only just this moment rang the doorbell. She leans in while humming, kneels down, carefully removes the slippers martyring his feet. He closes his eyes and lets himself slide down a bit on the sofa. He experiences feelings he cannot define. Relief? Gratitude? Affection? Love? This young woman who carefully removes his slippers, humming...

This, he says to himself, stunned, is what I live for.

BORN NOWHERE

In a café in P★, capital of F★, a young Moroccan approaches me quite civilly ("Are you really What's-his-name, the gazetteer?") and vehemently assures me that I must hear *his* story—he seems to have only one, like most people.

My first instinct is to flee.

But let's analyze the situation. October. Saturday. Beginning of the evening. The sky low and heavy outside weighs like a lid / and discourages strolls. So, may as well stay in the warmth, in this bar, opposite the church S★ G★ of P★, to hear what the young man has to say. Light years away from Café de l'Univers (so far, all that…), leagues from other locales, X (that's his name) recounts:

"A few months ago, in order to obtain my passport to come study in France, I had to give to the appropriate authorities, in Rabat, an official copy of my birth certificate, which I had received myself from the *moqaddem* of the area for a shiny new ten-dirham bill. Once in my hands, I passed on the aforementioned document, without even glancing at it, to the prefecture—those men, those women, the famous appropriate authorities."

"Not even glancing at it, you say?"

"Not even."

"Well, my dear friend, we can already predict the worst

catastrophes are in store for you. One must always read *everything* when it's an administrative affair. Down to the last word, every comma. And even between the lines."

"Perhaps. But I didn't pay any attention to the information in the document because I believed (naively) that I already knew the details."

A pause.

"After all, I know who I am, right?"

This was said in a defiant tone, the strands of his hair disheveled, his look somber. I, prudently:

"We say that, and then one day…"

He cut me off, vehemently:

"But no! Big mistake! We don't know who we are, monsieur! We know nothing, monsieur, no matter what Aristotle and all of philosophy have to say about it! When I received my identity card, I saw with stupefaction that after 'place of birth' came the response: 'Khzazna,' even though I believed I remembered—vaguely—having been born in Rabat."

"You *remember* your place of birth? That's a bit precocious."

He shrugged his shoulders.

"I mean to say that I've always more or less known that I was born in Rabat. Where did this strange Khzazna come from? It wasn't a series of typing errors, the letters in 'Rabat' and in 'Khzazna' aren't close on the keyboard. I verified—even a monkey typist, even a doddery drunkard, could not end up with 'Khzazna' while trying to type 'Rabat.' Or else, he would have to be flailing around in every which way…"

He leaned toward me, finger raised.

"I calculated the probability of getting 'Khzazna' while trying to type 'Rabat': one chance in one hundred thousand billion. On the human level, monsieur, it's an *impossibility!*"

"Excellently said."

"All this was bizarre. At that moment, I couldn't do anything, for I was preoccupied with my departure for France, which constitutes, as you know, a veritable obstacle course, with its pre-registrations, its registrations, its thousand certificates…But I remained intrigued by this story."

"Why not just forget about it?"

"Forget about it? It quickly became an obsession! After resolving a thousand problems related to settling in France, I reached a calmer period of my life; and, to be honest, happier. We are, after all, in one of the most beautiful cities in the world?"

"Mmm."

"One of the most interesting?"

"Hrmblmmmn."

"But all my friends at the Cité Internationale where I had set down my luggage, all my friends were born in prestigious places, such as Fes or Rabat or Marrakech, or at least interesting places, such as Azrou or Azemmour. But Khzazna? *Quès aco?* I kept a low profile, buckling under the weight of my shameful secret. And if they were to ask me where I had seen the light of day? Would I be able to lie?"

A waiter materialized above our table, haughty in black and white, and enjoined us to order something ("or else disappear," his scowl seemed to say). We ordered two coffees and he left, full of disdain. The young man resumed his story.

"Sometimes it was the opposite—I was caught up in a flash of exaltation and saw myself as a duke or at least a marquis, lord of a land perhaps inundated with history, and I was 'of Khzazna' as others are 'of La Rochefoucauld.' But the exaltation faded fast and I was rotting away once more in the agony of not knowing who I was, having been born nowhere. I needed to be sure! After research worthy of the best explorers, conducted at the Centre Pompidou and at the Bibliothèque Nationale on the rue Richelieu, after exhausting numerous road maps, I succeeded in locating this place where I had been born, at least in the eyes of the law. The pre-war Guide Bleu, unearthed at a secondhand bookstore, was adamant: Khzazna existed indeed!"

"That must have reassured you."

"It was a spot on a map!"

"That's better than nothing."

"Mmmmyeah. A Guide Bleu dating from the Protectorate, suffice to say from prehistoric times...So, a few months ago, during summer vacation, back in Morocco, I wanted to be sure. Without saying anything to anybody, I took the bus to Rabat and I went to see. I saw. In fact, Khzazna is not the name of any city, nor any village, nor any hamlet."

"A ruin, then? A poet's dream? At least a well?"

"No. It's a beautiful land fifty miles east of Rabat, a rather pleasant countryside where time stopped long ago—in the age of the Guide Bleu perhaps. It's swarming with cows, sheep, hens, and rabbits."

"So far, nothing extraordinary."

"Nothing extraordinary, certainly; but imagine my surprise

when I learned, after approaching a local gnome and asking him a few questions, that there wasn't even a hint of a hospital nor of a maternity ward in this place. There's only a free clinic in the small neighboring village, constructed two years ago. I'm a little bit older than that, after all."

He slouched in his chair, brow furrowed.

"The question you must be asking yourself now, that I asked myself a long time before you, is the following: where was I born, exactly? Between two trees? On a hill? There, next to the stream?"

"In a barn, like Jesus?"

"There wasn't a single barn in the vicinity. (Do you mind? It's my story.) When I returned to the house, in the grips of a great anxiety…"

"…of identity…"

"…I rushed to the kitchen and demanded that my mother enlighten me. She was kneading I don't know what in the half-light. A good minute passed before anything happened. Then she replied, seemingly unbothered, that I was born in the maternity ward of Rabat, like everyone else…"

"…but…"

"…but that my maternal grandfather had beseeched my parents to write the word "Khzazna" in the family records, in the appropriate box."

"The grandfather's always to blame."

"Indeed, but why? Why? You'll never guess in a million years."

"I give up immediately."

The waiter appeared and placed on our table, in a brusque gesture, two cups of coffee (tintinnabulating as they knocked against each other); then he left, full of arrogance. The young man leaned toward me once again, as if he were about to reveal the third secret of Fatima.

"All because, at the time, he would often run as a candidate in the local elections in the district of Khzazna! Elections he sometimes won, but with the tiniest lead: one vote, one alone, could make all the difference."

Now I really got into the discussion, my voice vibrating with incredulity (80%) and indignation (20%):

"You expect me to believe that in this land where there are only, according to you, cows, sheep, hens, and rabbits, they vote, they elect representatives of the people in real assemblies? There are congressmen? Councillors? County magistrates, perhaps?"

He drank a small sip of coffee then struck his fist against the table (an abundance of ! followed).

"Exactly, monsieur! There is all that and perhaps even more! Laugh as much as you like!"

"But…why?"

"The first governments after Independence wanted it that way, probably in order to balance the weight of Rabat, that nest of leftists who voted like one single man for Abdallah Ibrahim and his friends. As I just told you, there were so few voters in Khzazna that one sole vote could make the difference. For my grandfather, I then represented not his grandson newly landed on earth (*you-you-you!* ululated the women), but a potential elector who would vote for him when I came of age, *twenty-one years later.*"

I was flabbergasted.

"Twenty-one years later?"

"Indeed!"

"And they say Moroccans don't know how to plan for the long term?"

"Utter nonsense!"

"That they only live in the moment?"

"Baloney!"

Moved, we looked into each other's innermost depths, proud to be part of a people so concerned with the future, and we ordered a pomegranate juice to drink to the health of triennial, and even quinquennial, plans.

The waiter insolently asked us if we *really* intended to sip pomegranate juice after drinking coffee. He seemed to imply that we were sinning against the spirit of the place, against the P★sian custom, against all traditions. We told him to get lost, which he did with a majestic step.

However, the young man was worried. He started up again, in a melancholic tone:

"This story has plunged me into a state close to nervous breakdown. (Yes it has! Yes it has!) To learn first of all that I'm not who I thought I was, which is to say a Rabati; to get used to this new identity as a citizen of Khzazna; then discover that this identity that I had ended up accepting was itself a fiction; and that this fiction was a political manipulation designed by my own family…"

"We cannot be betrayed but by our own."

With a distracted finger he wiped the bottom of the pomegranate juice lingering in his glass; then he sucked his finger, becoming more and more heavyhearted.

"Well, I wasn't yet at the end of my troubles. That same night, while I confided the discovery of my precarious stateless state to my uncle Brahim, how did my uncle respond? Comforting words, a fitting *hadith*, encouragements? Not at all! He pushed me even further into my distress by revealing to me an even more bizarre fact that concerned me as well."

He squeaked:

"My own uncle!"

"Family, I tell you… But what did he say, exactly?"

"This: 'My dear nephew, not only were you born nowhere, but, in a certain way, you were never born at all.' Just like that!"

"Allow me to write that phrase in my notebook."

"'My dear nephew, not only were you born nowhere, but, in a certain way, you were never born at all.' And he went on to recount a detail that everyone had forgotten—except him."

"Uncles, they forget nothing."

"It's important to know that I was born (if we can call it being born) toward the end of December 1973. My father was summoned to a council where he was told the following: 'My dear Abdelmoula'—did I tell you that my father was named Abdelmoula?—'if you declare the birth of your son today, or even tomorrow, he will lug around for the rest of his life a year reduced to a few days. Everyone will think he's eight years old, when really he'll only be seven years and five days old. Better to wait for the beginning of the coming year and only then go bother the civil registrar.'"

"Understandable."

"For close to a week, and while I was wriggling about, innocent, in my diapers, nothing happened. I mean *officially*. In practice, my family probably slit the throat of some ram, or at least a rooster, and offered plates of couscous to the poor near the mosque; but I didn't yet exist on paper. In my diapers, yes; but on paper, no. Then, around the 2nd or 3rd of January, my father went triumphantly to announce my birth to the authorities. The authorities, who are used to—the imbeciles—believing the word of citizens, thus noted that a certain X★, son of Abdelmoula Y★, was born in Khzazna January 2nd, 1974."

"Fake birthplace, fake year! Bravo! You've got it all!"

"This avuncular revelation stupefied me. I went stumbling out into the night to wander in the little streets of Rabat. It was gorgeous outside…"

"Let's stick to the story."

"The question I was asking myself that night, stumbling in the streets, haggard, the question I'm still asking myself, is: *am I really myself if I was born elsewhere and the year before?*"

"Colossal enigma!"

We ordered another fruit juice to better meditate on life's uncertainties. The young man seemed to have calmed down, now that he had emptied his heart of past resentments, as if the confidence he had taken in What's-his-name was enough to appease him.

He glanced at the parvis in front of the church S★ G★ of P★. A tourism van had just unleashed tens of Japanese tourists who were agitating silently. A Comoran was selling hot chestnuts while two Tamils seemed to be surveying the area. A beggar, sitting on the steps of the church, was reaching an alms bowl toward the faithful entering into the house of God.

My one-night companion continued.

"What a truly superb city! I really think I'll end up becoming a citizen of P★. Let it take as long as it takes. At least that's an identity."

He got up and took off, just as civilly as he had approached me, after throwing a crumpled banknote on the table. I remained alone on my banquette.

Not for long: The famous Samir J★, passing by, noticed me through the window, entered the café, and came to join me, hoping I would buy him a drink.

After ordering, I quickly recounted the story I had just heard. J★ reflected for a bit, then cried out, slamming his fist on the table, as the citizen of Khzazna had done before him:

"This story proves what I have always believed. Identity problems don't exist. We create them! 'Who am I? Where am I going? What am I good for?'"

"'What state am I wandering in?'"

"Pointless questions! This young man doesn't realize how lucky he is. It's easy to say to yourself: *oh là là*, I was born nowhere, at no time, boo hoo, I'm so unlucky!"

He swallowed a mouthful of beer and continued.

"But the worst is to know precisely where you were born, and when, down to the very second; and despite that to have a *doubt*. A doubt based on certitude, that's the worst!"

"'A doubt based on certitude.' I don't understand that at all but it seems totally plausible to me. Allow me to write it in my notebook."

"I was born in Paris, in Baudelocque. If need be, I could find the room, the bed, the exact place, the stain on the ceiling. As for the day, I know it perfectly. The precise hour, the precise meter, everything is known, archived, fixed for centuries to come. So what?"

He brought his face close to mine, his teeth clenched.

"I don't know who I am any more than this dandy from Kaza Naza!"

"Khzazna."

"But at least he can imagine that an identity is *possible*. He can believe that if he rectifies something, two or three administrative trifles, a number, a name, everything will fall back into place. If he had really been born where the register said, the day it said, then there wouldn't have been any problem. So he can believe that, potentially, he doesn't have a problem! So, *deep down*, he doesn't have a problem!"

"Bravo! I understood nothing."

J★ shouted (one of his tics):

"However, what I'm saying is simple: identity problems, everybody has them! But they go much deeper than we think!"

"But a minute ago you were bellowing the opposite: 'Identity problems don't exist!'"

"It's the same thing!"

"You're contradicting yourself."

"Never! And in any case, I don't give a damn!"

I shouted even louder:

"Exactly, you old rascal!"

Then a young woman, a brown-hair-and-glasses whom I had crossed paths with two or three times at the Cité Internationale, approached us. She yelled at us:

"Messieurs, you're making a lot of noise," she remarked. "People are talking. Heads are turning and a *tsss tsss* is reverberating through the mink coats. And since you're mixing French and Moroccan, you're bringing shame to all of Morocco. And to me, as a result. Because I'm Moroccan..."

She grabbed a chair and sat down next to us.

"...even though I was born in Vietnam to a Russian father. Incidentally, am I really a woman?"

At that precise moment, we jumped up, Samir J★ and I, and disappeared, horrified, into the P★ian night.

We're still running, even now, fleeing from the immense flood of identity problems seemingly trying to submerge the world and its inhabitants, and we strongly suspect, as we gallop, that these problems are not any more real than those of the native-torn citizen of Khzazna.

"One day," Ali confided in us…

"Wait, let's order first."

(What are you going to have? I dunno…You? *etc.*)

Five minutes later:

"One day," Ali confided in us…

"*Or rather ooonnnnne night*," crooned Hamid.

"Stop, let him talk!"

"Good God! If we can't coo along…"

"Except you're not cooing innocently, you're doing it just to bother him."

"Me? You accuse me of being some kind of provocateur? *etc.*"

Five minutes later:

"It was last year. I was freelancing for *La Tribune de Casablanca*—we have to pay for our studies after all…"

"Sure, but hang on a second, someone must have pulled strings for you. One doesn't just become a freelancer for *La Tribune* like that."

"You think someone pulled strings for me? You accuse me of being some kind of bourgeois? *etc.*"

Five minutes later:

"One day, and this is what I've been trying to get to, one day,

I found myself in Khouribga, researching (get this) 'men who matter.' Bizarre, no? (And note that I'm talking about men, not women—freelancers aren't sent off to research icons or muses…"

"That wouldn't be a bad film title: *No muse for the freelancer.*"

"…nor the skilled kolkhoz women, even less the Cleopatras or the Kahinas, as if those tramps' counterparts didn't exist in the Cherifien Empire under Hassan II. But anyway.) You've asked me to *essplain.* It was a sudden whim of the director of *La Tribune.* Thumbs passed through the holes of his cardigan (he didn't have the money to repair the seams, you know how poor the gazettes are), so, fingers in the holes, a badly lit Casa Sports dangling from his disdainful lip, spectacles on his nose (à la "press boss"), he hit me with the following, at dawn: 'You're gonna do a piece for me on *men who matter…*'—utterly untimely—'…in Khouribga.' I didn't dare ask him what he meant by that. (A freelancer shuts up or gets out.) I wasn't so much worried by the strangeness of this inquiry: why the devil was *La Tribune de Casablanca* interested in what went on a hundred miles to the east, high up on this arid plateau where nothing grows except esparto and problems? I'm a freelancer, I don't bother myself with these considerations. So I rushed *pronto* to the bus station, I boarded a bus dating from before the Flood—held together only by a bolt, paint, and prayers—and after a trek which it's best you know nothing about (someone even vomited on me, a baby), I got off around noon in Khouribga, a dusty little town…"

"…with every intention of staying that way…"

"…where a cousin of mine had been wandering around the Tadla bitumen office for months. I quickly stumbled upon him, as he spent all his days in a café, hoping for employment that never came, but still living in hope. Emotional embraces, taps on the back, I'm fine, my brother, *hamdoullah*, and your mother, *hamdoullah*, and your sister, *hamdoullah*, fine, fine, thanks be to God, and the little Narjis, he's getting bigger, *hamdoullah*, and the old Allal, may God rest his soul, oh really? *ma cha'llah*, and the neighbor So-and-so, we hung him, and the cat, *etc.* Five minutes had passed when I suddenly remembered the reason for my expedition.

"'Hamou…,' I say to him."

"His name was Hamou?"

Ali ignores the senseless interruption.

"'Hamou, I say to him, I'm looking for *men who matter* in this town!' He nods, pours himself a cup of tea, sips the boiling beverage, brow furrowed, eyes half-closed, lost in thoughts as deep as 'the lake' of little Lamartine (do you remember, from high school?), thoughts so deep that one might worry he'd never return, lost in the world of Ideas (you remember, philosophy class?). Then he shakes himself…"

"What does that mean, 'he shakes himself'?"

"…he shakes himself like a horse and hits the palm of his hand on the table, with a male and resolute air. 'Ali,' he says to me, 'I know them *all*!'"

Sensation around the table.

"Happy times when one can know all the men who matter in Khouribga!"

"Today, the population has exploded in every direction. We're even in Italy!"

"We don't know our neighbor, monsieur!"

"We don't even know where we live!"

We finally kept quiet and regarded, eyes filled with emotion, our friend who was recounting this incredible adventure in such detail. During the explosion of commentary that interrupted his narration he was chomping at the bit, metaphorically speaking, all while caressing a cat; this cat submitted his derrière to him, as is the habit of cats, all while purring peacefully. The silence that had just fallen over Café de l'Univers invited Ali to resume his story.

"So Hamou tells me about many of these men who matter; he even has the courtesy to present them classified by category—my cousin is methodical, like all the Soussis. I note *in petto* what he reveals to me, thank him, take care of the bill (a languid tea, an insoluble coffee) and plunk myself on the sidewalk. Did I mention it was hot out? It was as if we were, as the poet said, 'under the torrents of a tropical sun.'"

"Which poet?"

"It doesn't matter, it's just an expression. The tropical sun, 'which spreads heat over our fallow lands.' What is to be done? as old Vladimir said. Let's begin with the entrepreneurs, I say to myself, mentally consulting my list, maybe there's a lunch to be had from it. I begin my rounds with Tijani, a prominent businessman, owner of a second-hand Bentley bought from an old crazy Tangéroise woman. I bribe the *chaouch* who keeps guard at the entrance of the building. He opportunely turns his gaze toward the road, shimmering with dust, while I climb a steep staircase; then I'm parleying with a panicked secretary in a sort of antechamber—I swear, it was as if she had never seen a journalist before, that young bird, much less a freelance journalist—one might even say she had never before seen a man, so much did she gawk, mouth agape—I try to dazzle her by presenting my fake press pass but does she even know how to read? Well, when she finally understands that I don't want her virginity, or her wallet, she goes to scratch at a door, pokes her head in, chirps…Long story short, Tijani receives me in a brand spanking new office, minimalist, in tones of gray anthracite, with a green plant in a corner that seems to keep watch. Tijani went to high school in Casablanca, some engineering school in France, then did his MBA at an American university—without tiring himself out, I might add—I would learn later that he's hypermnesic and a total idiot. He returned to the country, one wonders why, perhaps to make his mother happy, or else he did something stupid in the US (we'll save the slander for another time), so he returned to the country and created his company here, christened Tijani and Co., which incidentally is a bit boastful since he's alone in his office, with the green plant and the secretary in distress: Mr. Co. is conspicuously absent. Whatever it may be, I congratulate Tijani on his success. Bravo! He shows me, quite proud, the plans, graphs, and diagrams, the hyperboles and even a parabola—then proposes that I, for the sake of my article, meet his FD, his HRD, or even his XYZ (all gentlemen who I suspect only exist in his head, for I didn't see anyone in the hallways of Tijani and Co., except for, useless to repeat it, his trying secretary and his plant, haughty as a hidalgo). I suspect he is a mythomaniac, a high-flying crook, but it's too hot to clarify matters; and in the end, hey, as long as he doesn't eat my cookie or bother my wife what does it matter to me whether Tijani is a businessman or a scrounger? I have just enough time to ask him a question: '*Dis-moi*, Tijani...'"

"You addressed him with the informal *tu*?"

"At the time, everyone *tutoyer*-ed each other."

"Who's 'everyone'?"

"Everyone who knew how to read and write. And who spoke Moroccan."

"You're taking the piss out of us, *etc.*"

Five minutes later:

"So I ask him: 'Tell me, Tijani, how do you follow the cycles of demand, the needs of the consumers, the projections, all that?' His eyes widen. 'Or maybe it's your FD who takes care of it? Or perhaps your XYZ?' His eyes widen. 'Unless there's a secret journal here that monitors the market?' His eyes widen. 'But I go see Bouazza, of course!' he cries. 'For God's sake!' He can't disclose any more, he has to slip out for an important business lunch—to which he forgets to invite me, the pig. Here I am on the sidewalk, the sun dripping from the heights of the blue sky. *Qué calor!* as the Colombians say. As if we were in a hammam at rush hour. I wipe my forehead with the sleeve of my shirt. My next rendezvous is with the governor, Si Ahmed, one of those brilliant technocrats recently nominated by the king to the head of important cities. I go by foot to the prefecture. It's at the end of the avenue. The *chaouch* who stands guard before the imposing building starts chasing me like I'm some kind of scumbag, at least he's about to, pitchfork raised, murderous eye, when he understands that I purport, me, a simple citizen, to go see the governor; stop there! I brandish my fake press pass, decorated with the colors of the national flag, threatening, and pass myself off as a special correspondent of Basri—might

as well really go for it. Do you remember Driss Basri, who was
minister of the interior at the time? Yeesh…The sole utterance
of his name made men piss themselves; the sight of his face, from
a distance, made women faint from fear; and the *chaouch* fell like
flies when his emissaries presented themselves at the drawbridge."

We interrupt Ali.

"We were all alive then. Today's youth don't want to believe us.
They downplay it, the little bastards: come on, they say, he wasn't
so terrible, *your* Basri."

"*Our* Basri? The dogs!"

Ali was starting to get irritated.

"May I continue?"

"Go on, go on."

"So the *chaouch*, before perishing from terror, opens the front
door for me and from one moment to the next I find myself in
the office of Si Ahmed. His Excellency, who doesn't hate being
talked about, receives the hack journalist, the freelancer—but what
did he know of it?—with kindness. He is welcoming, certainly,
even courteous; but he is also a voluble visionary who deploys, to
my stupefaction, relief maps, perhaps of Vauban, on a big meeting table. His hands flutter about: he points out this, shows me
that, underlines, designates, regenerates, erases, constructs. He's
the demiurge, I swear! Next he shows me the aerial photos taken
by drones belonging to the US Air Force, which maybe didn't
even exist at the time; he speaks to me of phantastic, phantasmic
projects, perhaps even pharaonic, in any case there's a *ph* somewhere in there. He gets heated, he sweats, he evaporates, more and
more eloquent. Globalization is a game for him, his benchmark is

millions of dollars, he's met Bill Gates and slapped a Chinese man. All the same I end up interrupting: 'Si Ahmed, this is all great, *mais comment faites-vous...*'"

"Him you *vouvoyer?*"

"Yeah, because we were speaking in French, not Moroccan."

"Bizarre, *etc.*"

Five minutes later:

"'Si Ahmed, this is all great, but how do you stay up to date with what happens in your *wilaya?* I mean, at the level of the average citizen? Your regular guys?' His eyes widen. 'Or perhaps it's your secret police who take care of that?' His eyes widen. 'Or else, you stroll around incognito in your city, like Haroun Arachide did before in Baghdad?' The governor throws his arms to the sky, appalled by my ignorance. 'What do you mean, secret police? What are you talking about, Arachide? For everything I need to know, I consult Bouazza, of course!'"

"Again Bouazza?"

"The same. I don't have time to mark my astonishment, Si Ahmed gets up, rolls out his six feet and two inches, crushes my dextral and excuses himself: he has to welcome Darryl F. Zanuck to convince him to transfer Hollywood to Khouribga—or at least to make a branch of it there. An ancient taxi, the kind that stays at the same speed even when it's lost its wheels, quickly brings me to the Trade Union House where I meet the legendary Kafouyi..."

"Kafouyi himself?"

"...Kafouyi who directs the federation of local trade unions with an iron fist, Kafouyi who makes *Les Bitumes du Tadla* tremble when he raises his left foot, when he threatens to unleash..."

"Lightning, like Zeus?"

"…the famous *general strike* that will bring down global capitalism starting with Khouribga—it's only a beginning, let's continue the fight! The man, whom I telephoned from Si Ahmed's office, awaits me resolutely in front of the building that houses *The Trade Union*—be afraid, bosses! Militant handshake, virile pat, the man receives me as though we had stormed the Winter Palace together. I go to make my little provocation…"

"You dared provoke the famous Kafouyi?"

"I did."

"And you survived?"

"I did."

"Well well, my colonel, *etc.*"

Five minutes later:

"So, I set right about provoking the old Kafouyi of the *zmâlas:* 'Mr. Secretary General, you have been in power since the departure of the French, since the death of at least three popes, since the passing of the comet, that's a bit long, no? People are saying that you cut yourself off from the laboring masses, people are whispering that the Trade Union House is like the palace of Sleeping Beauty—people are protesting that nothing has changed since the year of Typhus. So (I clear my voice) how do you know what the state of mind is of your adherents?' His eyes widen. 'How do you decide when it's necessary to trigger a strike and when to stop it?' His eyes widen. 'How do you estimate the combativeness of your troops?' He gathers his brow, irritated by my insolence: 'I know very well what the workers are thinking, monsieur,' he quakes. 'All I have to do is talk to Bouazza!' Hell and damnation!

Again Bouazza? *Who he?* The large Kafouyi shows me to the door without ceremony, like a vulgar reformist, like the last of the Mensheviks, and without leaving me the time to ask him who he is, this famous Bouazza, to top it all off! Waiting for an unlikely taxi on the sidewalk, liquefied by the sun spreading over the city like a layer of magma, I think to myself that it's obviously this Bouazza I need to interview instead of wasting my time with second fiddles—whether they be unlikely CEOs or a megalomaniac governor or the king of the syndicates. He is the one who is, without a doubt, 'the man who matters' in Khouribga, the one who makes things happen, one of the *movers and shakers*, as we say in good French. Before going on the hunt, I needed to cool myself down (it was 104 degrees F) and get a haircut. Desperate, I play the semaphore and a Peugeot survived from the band of Bonnot stops before me. I throw myself in. I collapse. The taxi driver kindly helps me out. 'A good hairdresser? Well, you don't have a choice, there's only one in the city. It's Bouazza.'"

Consternation in Café de l'Univers.

"What? A hairdresser? Oh misery, deception!"

"Our illusions, crushed!"

"We thought at least *L'Orchestre rouge*…"

"…the Count of Saint-Germain…"

"…a bionic spy…"

"I am filled to the brim with astonishment. I would even say: flabbergasted. The taxi drops me off in front of the barbershop. I enter, a bit worried, but there's really no reason to be. The place resembles a hundred others, but the boss, the aforementioned Bouazza, doesn't resemble anyone else. Bland, gray on gray, the mustache of a field mouse…He extends a floppy hand, I am his first client of the afternoon, he informs me, and points me toward the chair where I am to perch myself. A sweeping glimpse around: a few guys sitting in chairs but, visibly, they are not clients, but rather friends, neighbors, the curious. No apprentice in sight, no associate. This Bouazza seems to do everything in his den: shampooer, delouser, hairdresser for women, hairdresser for men, colorist if the occasion presents itself, perms for the Polynesian dentist's wife washed up there no one knows how. Bouazza is a polyvalent figaro—as in, you ask him if he can do something, he responds: I can!"

"We all know someone like that."

"The man of agile hands starts to do his work, his fingers ferret about in my hair, searching for the rebel cowlick, and I set about learning the central role he seems to play in the capital of bitumen. I don't double cross him, I put all my cards on the table: I cut the deck with the governor, I declare Tijani, I lay down Kafouyi. He, the capillary artist, nods, ambling through my hair; doesn't say a word but nods; and when I've finished, as the prose writer said, he remains silent for a moment, contemplating his oeuvre inversed in the mirror: he did a sort of monk tonsure that was very à la mode, *àlamoude*, he affirms—for example, from the times of cathedrals—then finally responds to the question I had asked him. Correct, he says, correct: all these characters are his clients.

"'And it's you,' I dared, 'who informs them of what goes on in their fair city?'"

"He wipes his hands on a rag dating from the year of the unicorn. The three or four bumpkins seated along the wall had not

61

yet opened their mouths—like a brochette of half-wits waiting to be devoured by a giant. Then he gives a faint smile, like a grin *putting on airs*, and finally he murmurs:

"'Me? But I know nothing of what goes on here… I never leave this shop, which I inherited from Mr. Ceccaldi, who was the hairdresser at the time of the French. I was his apprentice.'

"And then the brochette of half-wits starts up in unison:

"'Bouazza never leaves this shop. He inherited it from Mr. Ceccaldi, who was the hairdresser at the time of the French. He was his apprentice.'

"My heart skips a beat out of fright, or perhaps from surprise. What is this cinema—or rather this ancient theater, with choir and coryphaeus? I get up, shove a few crumpled bills in the hand of the artisan, who verifies the amount with a glimpse of the eye—*l'oeil du maître*—then pockets them without saying a thing. I don't know why, I feel a strong desire to slap him but I restrain myself, for these events are bigger than me and I find it all very tiresome. Well, it's decided, I'll leave this incomprehensible town—after all, my article is written. I start running, on the big avenue I stop an old Strindberg car, and I slump into a beat-up seat. The road that leads to Casablanca snakes around the plateau that shines with a thousand fires, *etc.* (I'll describe it another time). I have a moment to think, between two deviations in the road. And it's then that I *understand*."

"You understand the deviations?"

"No. I understand this story of Bouazza the hairdresser, who calls to mind a cretin from the Atlas, who most certainly is a cretin, and a beautiful one, and yet, it's in his den where conflicts are mitigated, it's in this insignificant place, essentially empty…"

"That reminds me of the Tao: *The spokes of the wheels converge at the hub. They converge toward the empty space. And it's thanks to the empty space that the chariot advances.*"

"Oh yeah, yeah, there's another: *The vase is made of clay but it's the empty space that makes it a vase.*"

"So, continuing on: It's in this insignificant, essentially empty place that the way of the world is negotiated between the authorities, the futile people, Kafouyi, the businessmen, *etc.* War, devastation…"

"Again with the deviation."

"No, I said: devastation, *dev-uhhh-stay-shin.*"

"Apologies."

"War, devastation, the struggle of everyone against one, or even *everyone against everyone*, all that is resolved at the barber's. There, each person unloads, without giving the impression of doing so, his observations, his demands, his remonstrances, his conditions, his numbers, his statistics. The choir—these bumpkins who have nothing else to do between two harvests other than populate Bouazza's cavern—the choir records it all and makes it into a refrain. The governor, the businessman, the trade unionist, the journalist take a seat in turn in the armchair, and at the end of the day, it creates a permanent negotiation. And it's thus that we are a *nation.* Because we all accept this incessant palaver at Bouazza's."

"Isn't it Renan who wrote something like '*What is a nation?*'"

"We've had the answer for a long time. We are a nation because, despite our differences of opinion, we all find ourselves at Bouazza's."

"We are smarter than Renan."

"On the other hand, he wouldn't have given me a monk's tonsure."

"Certainly not…"

"…àlamoude."

And on this lovely afternoon ("golden brown," "glowing," *etc.*); on this lovely afternoon when time seemed to stand still, as if awaiting its hour, when we claim the sun stops its trajectory ("have I really been following its course all this time?") for a few moments, just before plunging behind its horizons ("bluish,""distant," *etc.*), leaving man as an orphan of its light and uncertain of tomorrow; so, in this lovely Casablancan afternoon, in the middle of the crowd ("colorful,""rushed") invading the paths of the park, we looked at each other, moved; and in the same gesture, with the same energy, in this Café de l'Univers where, after our ramblings, we discovered certain laws ("the Laws of the Universe"), we raised our empty glasses to the memory of Ernest Renan and to that (future) one of Bouazza, to the longevity and vitality of our beautiful nation—and, above all, above all, to the empty space perfect in its milieu, the incredibly beautiful empty space that one sometimes has the desire to bow before and kiss on its hands—even the rain, even autumn, doesn't have such delicate hands; the empty space so opportune, so violent and so efficacious, that it's thanks to it, and only it, that the chariot (of the State) advances—that our cows are well guarded—and that our banner flaps in the wind, proud, haughty, and perfectly useless.

WHAT WAS NOT SAID IN BRUSSELS

"Brussels," murmured John…

…and something in him whispered: "Funny place to meet up." They were irritating, these set phrases that surged on the current of his thoughts. In this case, he knew where the expression came from. A film, of course. A French film, with Deneuve and Depardieu. But more often than not he didn't know where these stray fragments came from, but they were there, suddenly, clearly stated, floating in the intimate monologue that accompanied John from morning till night, a wave of words he could only escape by closing his eyes and listening to a sonata ("Again with your Bach!" sighed Annie…). An article caught his attention in the *Volkskrant* he had just bought in the Amsterdam train station and was now reading while waiting on the platform for the Thalys departing for Brussels. Scientists had made "a giant step" in *mindreading*. More irritation. Why were they talking about progress (a step is progress, isn't it?) when science made an advance—hmm, "an advance…"—when science made an incursion (an intrusion) in people's heads? John tried to inculcate a sense of perspective in his students at the University of Amsterdam: yes, science is still the most precious thing man has ("And art, m'sieur?"—he had chosen to ignore, for once, Guusje and her little face riddled with freckles, eternally questioning everything…), yes, science, it's what separates us from barbarism, but (he had raised an imperious finger) limits must be established!

He finished the *Volkskrant* article and the Thalys still hadn't arrived. He consulted his watch then began an imaginary course for the ectoplasms: "What does that mean, 'to read the thoughts of Mr. Tartempion'? All I had to do was think of Brussels and the phrase 'funny place to meet up' formed mechanically in my head. Where does this idiocy come from? We don't know! From physicochemical connections in the spongy mass we call the brain, from an electric shock…It all happened automatically, as if I had inadvertently pushed a button programmed, unbeknownst to me, to open a hidden door. (A sweeping glance around the lecture hall to check that his students had understood the image.) To what extent am I, *me*, responsible for that chain of events?"

The Thalys pulled in noiselessly along the platform. John steered himself toward car 11, in front of which stood an affable employee who took a glance at his ticket.

"Seat 74, on your right," said the employee in Dutch and then French.

John contented himself with nodding his head and giving a faint smile. He had stopped making remarks along the lines of "Yes, I know, I take this train two times a month" a long time ago, for they accomplished nothing, except, perhaps, an irate reaction from the employee ("Excuse me for trying to be of service…"). He had decided, once and for all, to consider each civil functionary as a machine with which it was necessary to maintain relations that our descendants will maintain with their South Korean robots:

informative, brief, concrete—never any affect or emotion. ("But, m'sieur, you're dehumanizing the world." "That happened long before I came along, mademoiselle Guusje.") Placing his suitcase above seat 74, John resumed his course: "Even if we get to that point one day, by implanting the most advanced electrodes in Mr. Tartempion's brain, to 'read' his thoughts, how would we separate those that belong to him of his own right, those that engage him and genuinely express his 'ego,' from those that appear all of a sudden, that do nothing, so to speak, but pass through?"

He plopped onto his seat, adjusted it to the reclined position, closed his eyes and continued. Addressing Stephan, one of his favorite students, he said: "Suppose I watch our Great Leader on the television—assuming we are in a totalitarian country— and this incongruous phrase forms in my head: 'Get out of here, fat-ass!' because at school, that's what we shouted at one of our classmates who was a little chubby and the Great Leader had put on some weight in the past few months…So, Stephan, you are a functionary of the Ministry of Control of the People's Thoughts and the electrodes are informing on me. The brain of citizen John Van Duursen, at 8:56pm, was crossed by the words 'Get out of here, fat-ass!' at the moment when our glorious Guide appeared on the little screen—so, Stephan, the question is: Am I responsible for this concatenation of words that formed without my being able to do anything about it?"

The Thalys had just set off and was now gliding out of the station, with the city on the left and the port on the right. "*Il y a des marins qui naissent / dans la chaleur épaisse…*", the song popped into John's head; he very much admired the great Jacques Brel.

Look who was adding grist to his mill now ("So to speak," thought John, vexed at not having anyone to whom he could remark that to add grist to the mill of a Batavian was certainly as pointless as supplying coal to Newcastle or sand to the Sahara).

"Looks like I got a little derailed there," he said—and he heard the phrase: "You mean, a little detailed?" Ha, ha. Here we have the clear proof of his theory: our thoughts don't belong to us, for the most part. They fall under the jurisdiction of...what's the phrase? Ah yes: spontaneous generation. They are little electric currents that...Anyway. He dove back into his magazine. The phrase "funny place to meet up" was all the more incongruous because he knew perfectly well why he was going to Brussels: to put an end to his relationship. Funny place to break up.

★★★

Annie hasn't smoked for a long time. She renounced her vice for John, her *Hollandais* (*"No, Annie, Holland is only a province of the Netherlands. I am né-er-lan-dais."*)...her capricious *Néerlandais*, a bit stubborn, terribly intelligent. She doesn't smoke anything and so much the better, for there is no longer anywhere to "light up"— she learned that expression from John—in the Gare du Nord, where she is waiting for the Thalys that will take her to Brussels. For the first time in months, her fingers are itching for it, she bites her lips, this would be the moment to exhale her anxiety in the cigarette's smoke. She raises her eyes toward the board that she's consulted a thousand times since the start, two years ago, of her long-distance relationship with the great Batavian she is about to meet in the land of Tintin.

The train leaves in fifteen minutes. I have time to go buy a newspaper. A bit more than an hour and I'll be in Brussels. It's curious, he didn't seem surprised when I proposed we spend the weekend there, instead of meeting up, per usual, in Paris or Amsterdam. He didn't ask any questions…What would I have replied? We began this adventure in Brussels, it's logical (she hesitates, perhaps that's not the appropriate word), it's *right* (suitable? appropriate?) that we separate there, like a loop closing itself, at once finished and infinite. How will John react to the decision she had made? To break up.

Car 17. After leaving her suitcase at the entrance, Annie goes to sit in the seat indicated on her ticket, discreetly stuffs Quies earplugs in her ears—no interest in hearing the multilingual jabbering of her neighbors—and takes out her newspaper. "The Dominique Strauss-Kahn affair" continues. It's a godsend for the press, whose sales are exploding. Everyone has an opinion on the topic. As it happens, it was the cause of her latest fight with John. Fight? Let's say snag, a cultural misunderstanding… "This type of scandal wouldn't happen in my country," John had decreed with that little air of moral superiority that frustrated Annie so much.

"That's right, treat us like degenerates while you're at it."

"Oh, don't exaggerate. You know I adore France. But come on, you let everything slide with your male politicians."

"Yours don't interest anybody, that's why we don't go digging through their private lives. Who ever heard talk of Balkenende or Rutte?"

It wasn't the first time they had quarreled, but that time had left a sour taste in her mouth. Was it possible to spend one's life with someone who always assumed the role of moral authority? A man she believed she loved but who irritated her with his obsessive reduction of everything to the following certitude: he knew what was right and she had no choice but to come around to his opinion. The Thalys was trundling now through the Parisian suburbs before reaching its tremendous speed in the plains of the north. "It's hard enough with each of us living in our own country, to always have these three hours of train between us," she thought. "If on top of that I have to live in a sort of permanent guilt because I don't have the Calvinist principles of Monsieur…" She remembered that John Calvin was French but didn't know how to turn the phrase to her advantage. Oh, whatever…Her eyes lingered again on the headline of her daily. Look at that, Johnny Hallyday is playing the actor, on the stage. In a play by Tennessee Williams, no less. She dreamed for an instant about going to see it with John but collided with another one of his principles: a play is done in the language in which it was written. Easy to say, when you're a polyglot like him. I'm a professor of history, not letters. I prattle through a bit of English. Thankfully he speaks my language. Ah, another theme of our squabbles. Whenever the opportunity arose, he would partake in long conversations in Dutch, in Amsterdam, in a café or at the home of friends, unconcerned that she didn't understand a word.

"You just have to learn Dutch."

"When, where, how? And why? All Dutch people speak English. And all I can make out is the *ghr*s and the *kh*s in that variety of sub-German."

In that instance, he was the one who got angry. First of all, Dutch was its own language, not a dialect. And it was the richest language in the world. Yes, madam! He had insisted on showing her, shaking with anger, the twenty or twenty-two volumes of the great dictionary of the Dutch language, "with more entries than the *Oxford English Dictionary* or the *Grand Larousse*." The quarrel lasted hours.

She tells herself she'll go light a votive candle at the church of Sainte-Catherine, in that pretty neighborhood in the center of Brussels, once she's no longer with John. She's not at all religious, but that would be a way to close the chapter. When the votive candle has been burned through, the relationship will have been utterly burnt out. Or else the reverse?

★★★

They had agreed to meet on the Place Jourdan, in a big hotel recommended by a diplomat friend. When Annie entered, she saw John sitting on a vast patio decorated with works of art and lit up by a skylight. She was impressed with the place. John had already checked in and was holding the room key in his hand. They kissed on the cheek like strangers. In any case, John didn't like public displays of affection. He brought her to the seventh floor ("seventh heaven, it's over," she thought with a pang of emotion…) and showed her with slightly melancholic pride the modern and comfortable suite with a beautiful view of Brussels. They struggled to recognize a few monuments in the distance. She was afraid he would want to take her in his arms, but he contented himself with waiting for her in the little living room, sitting on the sofa while she dropped off her things in the bedroom. She made a quick tour of the bathroom (everything was perfect) and then returned to the living room. In a cheerful tone she asked:

"So, what should we do now?"

The same thought crossed their minds: "Now's not the time."

"Have you eaten lunch?" (She nods, she had a sandwich on the train.) "Alright, let's take a walk, it's not even two o'clock yet, we'll decide about dinner later."

"Where should we go?"

"While I was waiting I took a look in the guide. There's a big park close by. We'll go take a walk through there?"

(*Fine, as usual, he's the one who decides, but it's the last time.*) They left the hotel, turned left and started down rue Froissart, then down rue Belliard. It was splendid out. That time, neither of them commented on the façades and their typically *bruxellois* alignment combining styles and epochs "with no regard for harmony," he normally said, "but which in any case has a certain something," she would then reply, "a *je-ne-sais-quoi*..."

"Ah yes, the *je-ne-sais-quoi*, the very practical French invention for when one runs out of arguments," he had said one day, snickering.

"Not at all, it's the expression of a subtle sentiment, almost... ineffable," she had replied. "Your mind is too practical to feel it."

He didn't like when she teased him.

"That's it, I'm just too...how do you say it, *fruste*? *Frustre*?"

"*Frustre* doesn't exist, it's a barbarism. The correct word is *fruste*."

"You think I'm unsophisticated? Because I don't know what

the I-don't-know-what is?"

He had laughed, rather satisfied with his play on words. She had replied, smiling, but with a dash of irritation:

"You are the most intelligent and most cultivated man I know. But come on, it's true that there's something quite Dutch about you. You yourself taught me the expression 'merchant and pastor.'"

"Yes, *koopman en dominee*. We still have a bit of that in our mentality. So?"

"So, neither the merchant nor the pastor is reputed for his sense of nuance, of ambiguity, of the in-between…"

That day he had laughed and left it at that. Today, Annie gazed with a bit of sadness at the façades of the buildings on the rue Belliard. It was the last time she would see them in John's company. Would she see them again one day? Would she have a reason to come back to Brussels and to this business district where tourists never venture? Everything around her seemed to be saying goodbye.

Five minutes later, they entered the Parc du Cinquentenaire. Contrary to their normal habit, they didn't hold hands and even avoided touching. "How will I tell him? What explanation will I give?" This silence that simultaneously separated and united them began to weigh on Annie. She pointed out a tree in the distance:

"Did you see that magnificent maple?"

John turned in the direction Annie was indicating, her hand extended toward a corner of the park, and hesitated an instant. Then he nodded his head without saying anything and plunged back into his thoughts. Trees…At the beginning it had been a delight to discover their names in the two languages, to touch a chestnut tree and exclaim at the same time, laughing: "*Marron-nier!*" "*Kastanjeboom!*" or "*Chêne!*" "*Eik!*" "Eik???" She had laughed herself to tears. What a funny name…"*Hêtre!*" "*Beuk!*" "Beuk??" "Come on, are you naming your trees or insulting them?" He had forced a laugh. And then, little by little, over the course of their walks, another feeling had surfaced. Sometimes he thought nostalgically of his previous relationships, with Petra or Mieneke, when it sufficed to name a tree, a flower, a fruit, without having to translate, so that right away, for both of them, a taste, a color, a childhood memory came to mind—and often the memory was the same, or nearly, the first orange tasted at Christmas, the striking appearance during a bike ride of an oak tree with its branches full of snow in the unreal silence of a winter morning, frozen and luminous, the first flowers to bloom in the garden of the family house, which bore a striking resemblance to the house that Petra or Mieneke had grown up in…With Annie, things were different: trees formed a sort of wall between them, the flowers spoke another language, fruit had the taste of another childhood, of another life. And all of that was lost…*Lost in translation*: It was the perfect phrase. It was a foregone conclusion: he had just seen the film…

Over the course of their walk, several such phrases formed in his head. "What am I doing here?" She was an old acquaintance, to whom he no longer even paid attention. The anxieties of ado-lescence…Yes, granted, no one knows why they are thrown into this ("cruel," of course) world, we can lie to ourselves, believe in endless rubbish, imagine ourselves chosen, invent gods and great designs, but at the root of it all, we don't know anything. So what?

What does it matter if life does or doesn't have meaning, as long as it has flavor? Another inscription surged from who knows where: "Who is this woman next to me?" Oh, he could have filled out a police report, he knew her name, her birthday, certain details that might be of interest for an anthropomorphic survey—and after? Would he have exhausted her? "It's been a while since you wore her out." Who said that? What boor? In the curve of a path, he had seen these words: "One must know how to end a strike." Curiously, the phrase was written in French; it took him a few moments to recognize it. Yes, it was the phrase that Annie had taught him, one of those quotations she had forced him to repeat, the good history professor, "because France is that, too, not just monuments and nice little meals, but also proclamations, slogans engraved into the French imagination and which now form a part of our soul, our collective unconscious—to understand us, you must learn them by heart…"—but where did that declaration come from? Ah yes, that former communist leader—John furrowed his brow—who? Yes, Maurice Thorez: "One must know how to end a strike." But why did he think of that? What was the connection? The words started to dance, then to glimmer and he saw that now they were saying something else: "One must know how to end a relationship." Who is speaking? Are they giving me an order? A piece of advice? Is it me talking to myself? In a language other than my own? Bizarre…

Their steps had carried them toward the museum of the Cinquantenaire. They stopped a moment to look at the great building, somber and solemn. They found themselves climbing up the majestic steps quite naturally. John mumbled something, she nodded yes and he went to buy two tickets. "What am I doing here?" she asked herself.

They walked through the rooms exchanging a few formulaic phrases. ("It's incredible how rich this museum is! — Yes...Why isn't it better known? You never hear anyone talk about it. Did you see those marble statues? — Fabulous!") Little by little, the phrases became less conventional, or else they took on a new meaning, as the museum closed in on them and its richness took on an extraordinary effect. The *Mosaïque de la Chasse* from Apamée in Syria, which the guide specified "came from the palace of the governor of *Syria Secunda*, a Roman province," left them speechless. Annie summed it up in one of her reflections that she sometimes made aloud and regretted just as soon, qualifying them herself as "Poujadist."

"I say, well, the governor of *Syria Secunda* did all right for himself!"

She had had to explain the word *poujadiste* to John a few months earlier...

The bronzes of Lorestan gave John an opportunity to speak of his time backpacking through Iran during his studies. "It was before the ayatollahs..." Annie remembered she had admired the beautiful samples at the Cernuschi museum in Paris.

"Samples of the ayatollah?"

"No, nitwit, of the bronzes!"

They burst out laughing, nervously, then became serious again, he a bit melancholic, she on the verge of tears. To get a hold of herself, she started reading aloud entire phrases from the guide. Since they were alone in the museum, she felt like she was strolling through an immense palace, as if it were their home. Her home. "The Egyptian collection contains more than eleven thousand pieces," she read. She showed him the "Dame de Bruxelles," then the relief of Queen Tiyi. He nodded his head without teasing her about her very recent knowledge. "The Roman collections are structured around a few important oeuvres: remarkable Etruscan mirrors, marble busts of the imperial epoch..." Leaning over the immense model of Rome, they showed each other, with their fingers, the monuments they recognized.

"That will be our next trip!" exclaimed Annie rashly—then she bit her lip.

In another room, they saw icons, silks, Coptic textiles, and Byzantine ceramics.

"*Mais c'est Byzance...*" Annie murmured mechanically.

John approached her.

"What did you say?"

Annie hesitated a bit then turned toward him and taught him the expression she had heard so often in her childhood. Her grandfather, in Toulouse, would come close to the table during parties, a big smile lighting up his emaciated face that had known so many hardships and he would exclaim, full of sun and kindness: "*Mais c'est Byzance!*"

"How would you say that in Dutch?"

He started to think.

"Het is de hoorn des overvloeds, maybe. But there's probably a better translation. I'll think about it..."

The Vietnamese ceramics, the Khmer sculptures, the drums from Laos plunged John into his childhood haunted by echoes of the war in Indochina on the radio…An imposing sculpture, brought from Easter Island, lured them toward a somber corner of the museum. Speechless, they lingered for several minutes before the menacing colossus without realizing they had drawn nearer to each other and were almost touching. The neighboring rooms presented the Inca, Mayan, and Aztec civilizations. Annie leaned in and read the texts diligently. John preferred to look first at the objects at length, then throw a rapid glance at the little cards glued to the displays. Annie murmured:

"…the feather-working art of the Indians of the great Amazon forests…"

She burst out laughing. John started to smile and looked at her, intrigued.

"No, it's nothing, it's a word that made me laugh: *plumassier*. I don't know it. It made me think of *plumard*. *L'art du plumard…* Bed art…It's funny."

John didn't laugh. "*Vind je dit grappig?*" He saw the words float before his eyes with the French translation: "*Et vous trouvez ça drôle?*" which he knew because one day Annie had made him listen to a sketch by Coluche which had ended in those words. Again another thing that didn't work: she never laughed at his witticisms. By the time he explained them, dissected them, they had obviously lost all their appeal. "You're terribly serious, you don't have a sense of humor…" Petra and Mieneke, on the other hand, had appreciated his deadpan humor, the little absurdities he delivered with a very serious air. Again, it was necessary first to understand them…

Inside the museum, he discovered a Gothic cloister. They sat for a moment on the cold stone. They had promised, one day, at the beginning of their adventure, to visit all the cloisters in all the abbeys of Europe… "A vast undertaking." "Yes, I know, I was waiting for that," thought John, hearing the voice of de Gaulle whispering his words to him. "I'll go alone to the cloisters," Annie said to herself, "maybe I'll put on a little black veil, they'll think I'm a penitent…" She pulled herself together. "What do I have to atone for? This is nuts! There's a part of me that feels guilty…" They left the cloister, took a wrong turn and found themselves in an immense room of pre-Columbian art. They were standing looking at a sort of miniature totem pole when John suddenly felt himself assailed by a tide of colors and sounds. Words formed in his head, it was as if he were a spectator looking on as it happened, and he distinctly heard his voice pronounce this phrase, in French:

"Annie, I'm sorry but it's over between us."

Immediately he felt a chasm open beneath his feet. No! He wanted to take back his words but it was impossible. The words were no longer there, there were only garish images, colors, echoes that bored into his skull. Terrified, he turned toward Annie but she was no longer at his side. Feverishly, he looked around the big room then saw her in the distance, her back to him. She was on the other side of the room, frozen before a display. He approached her, wondering how she had managed to walk away without him hearing. He touched her shoulder, she gave a start and turned around, shaken, shocked, looking haggard. But it was impossible, she couldn't have heard him. Why this fright, then? He noticed a sort of gray mummy in the display. It was a terrifying skeleton, an adolescent embalmed in a strange position, as if crouching.

His bones were distinctly visible, one could make out the pieces of skin now turned to leather, one could surmise his gaze in his sunken eye sockets. Annie nestled herself in John's arms and started to cry.

Now they were too tired to go admire the glassware, the stained glass windows, the tinware, and the ceramics the guide promised in the chapel. The lacework, the textiles, the clothing...

"Another time," she said.

"Yeah," he responded. "*I shall return.*"

"Why are you speaking in English?"

"It's actually a famous saying. It's what General MacArthur said while leaving the Philippines under the threat of the Japanese, during the war."

"Do you know how to talk other than in quotations? Do you know that you're extremely tiring? And for starters, it's not *I shall return* but *We shall return.*"

She had said all that with a lot of tenderness. They returned to the hotel, making a detour to pass under the archway of the Cinquentenaire. This time, in the park, their hands searched for each other, found each other. Back at the hotel, they went to have a drink at the restaurant bar. They decided together to stay there for dinner instead of going to the Grand Place, as John had planned. The waitress was Italian, friendly, and discreet. Annie took a sip of wine and remarked:

"You're certainly quiet, for once!"

He smiled, took her hands and looked her in the eyes. He said nothing, but the words jostled around in his head.

"Today, I almost lost you...But I realized that all the phrases that brought me toward our separation…toward what I thought was *my* decision to separate, were not from me…In a certain way, I heard voices. Quotations. Words, collars of sounds that came from I don't know where. When you were getting on my nerves, I saw phrases appear. 'What an idiot!' 'What am I doing with this woman?' 'This relationship isn't going anywhere.' 'Let's finish it!' Words…But the important thing is that atrocious feeling of solitude that gripped me *in a second* when I thought it was over. That was concrete. That was *me*. My body, my soul, call it what you will…It's then that I understood, at that precise moment. (By what miracle did you walk away from me when I thought you were by my side?)"

She looked at him with a sardonic air, thinking: "You'll never know it, but I came to Brussels to break up with you. It's too complicated, this long-distance relationship. And your *hollandais* character…sorry, *néerlandais*. And then, it's stupid but…It was while looking at that mummy that I said to myself: he is alive. You, I mean…He's full of faults, obsessions, he gets on my last nerve sometimes, but it's precisely *that* which makes him alive. It's that spark of life, even if it expresses itself through a bad temper, that I'm in love with. I know that now. We will visit all the cloisters of all the abbeys in the world."

The delicious dishes that came one after another unknotted their tongues. It was almost midnight when they got back to the seventh floor. He stepped aside to let her enter the suite then entered in his turn. He closed the door, softly, almost tenderly, aware that he was entirely inside of this act. And in all those that

were to come.

BENNANI'S BODYGUARD

Nagib puts down *Le Matin du Sahara*, looking preoccupied, subsumes us in his detestation of the world in one glance, and bursts out:

"What are autoimmune diseases?"

Prudently, we keep quiet. The question seems to evoke others. A discussion might break out, medical, mean. It's hot, Saturday morning, Maure's cat (the boss's cat? To whom does this wretched cat belong? And can a cat belong to someone in the first place?), the cat of Café de l'Univers sleeps, rolled in a ball, on a neighboring chair. The passersby pass, hurried, because we are in Casablanca, and not in Tafraoût, and because we must look hurried, even if we have nothing to do, to allay suspicion, to convince others that we're up to snuff, that we're true Casablancais, busy, industrious, useful—not like those Marrakchi clowns, who do nothing the livelong day, nothing at all but stare at a big ochre minaret and tell jokes.

The silence thickens like cotton wool soaked with the blood of the poor.

So Nagib changes his tactic. He points his finger at Hamid and repeats his question, which becomes comminatory:

"What are autoimmune diseases?"

Hamid, attacked, first defends himself by pretending to be deaf, then mute, then an idiot, which for him isn't difficult. But nothing was able to divert the rage of knowledge that had taken hold of Nagib. He repeats his question, louder.

Dadane, who joined us this morning, swoops (half-heartedly) to Hamid's aid.

"Autoimmune diseases? It would take too long to explain, and would require, in addition, pencils, paper…But, instead, I'll tell you the story of Bennani's bodyguard…"

Everyone raises their eyes, even those (Hamid) who earlier had pretended not to have them. Collective astonishment:

"Did you say 'bodyguard'?"

The Moor draws closer, noting our awakening, sensing consumption. We rapidly order mint teas, a coffee, a Mekka cola.

"Did you say 'bodyguard'?"

Dadane settles into his cramped chair, clears his throat, takes on a tone of "I'm about to tell you something really amazing," and jumps in:

"Toward the end of 19**, high school students in the advanced math class in the Lycée Lyautey in Casablanca (I among them) decided to organize a little celebration, to celebrate…to celebrate what, exactly? I don't remember. But it doesn't matter…"

"There aren't that many reasons to be happy, we won't be finicky. Continue."

"The students were perhaps commemorating the demonstration of a theorem?"

"Ha ha, very funny…Anyway, they rented a room on Boulevard

Mohammed V, a space pompously christened 'the celebration room' by the proprietor. In reality it was a type of big hall that took on a festive spirit and whose walls, *bounni*-colored, oozed despair. The ceiling was strung with large banners that had been placed there for another occasion (the creation of a union) and that someone had forgotten to take down. So what, we would celebrate beneath partisan slogans—it would take more than that to ruin the commemoration of Thales' theorem."

"Thales is imperturbable."

"Irrefutable."

"Sent to do some reconnaissance, Anouar had accepted the owner's conditions. He was the one who had described the room to us, but, prudent, he had spoken of pink walls: we didn't know what the color *bounni* was. Pink walls! Old Thales would be turning in his grave with glee. Greeks like pink (don't they?)."

We didn't respond, we were no Hellenic experts.

"Stocks of drinks were purchased: Coca-Cola, Youki of course, Sim, Sinalco, and other brands that have completely disappeared from the surface of the planet."

"No alcohol?"

"Yeah, a bit of beer. Discreetly. These were the days when you could drink beer without triggering a heavy fire of *fatwas*, without provoking questions from Parliament, without upsetting the Pakistanis in the distance."

"Joyous age!"

"When the day came, we gave ourselves a close shave, perfumed ourselves with a ten-franc Spanish perfume, and walked gaily to the celebration hall to save the price of a bus ticket (1 dirham and

20 centimes). We put on our least shabby clothes, our least dusty shoes, our least nominal ties. Thales's band traversed Casablanca as if it were a conquered city."

"The world is ours!"

"After walking for a half hour…We had arrived! But what, what's going on, the door is closed! We hung around in front of the hall because that imbecile Mourtada had forgotten the key in the pocket of his everyday pants, which he wasn't wearing today, by definition: he was in his Sunday best, even if it was Friday night. He went running back down Boulevard Ziraoui to look for the key. We waited for him on the sidewalk (there was no danger, these weren't the days when extremists came to blow themselves up in a crowd as soon as they noticed a gathering of more than three people)."

"Happy days!"

"Joyous age!"

"So we wait peacefully, talking about Hilbert spaces and Max-well's equations. But…a black BMW pulls up in front of us. Do I need to describe a BMW? It's a German-made car, particularly well designed and with a powerful engine. It's a gem of that advanced technique that will always squash the beggar."

"We know what a BMW is. We've seen them. From a distance."

"Bennani gets out (from the black BMW). Bennani was the rich kid in the advanced math class. Rather nice, intelligent, generous on occasion, his only fault was that he was rich and we weren't. Normally, all he had to do was appear to send us, by contrast, back to our sad condition of 'sons of the masses.' (It was the time when even the sons of the masses could go to the Lycée Lyautey in Casablanca.)"

"Happy days!"

"Joyous age!"

"But that day, he couldn't outdo us. We were in our best threads. Or rather: our most decent threads. Even our nominal ties could bear the comparison with his satin lavalliere with one dangling button. We felt like we could stand up to Bennani. On this sidewalk where we were loitering, we held our heads high, proud to be as well dressed as he. Dadouche had even borrowed a suit from his cousin. So he took a step toward Bennani, ready to defy the gaze of the nabob math wiz.

"'Monsieur, we shall fight!'

"'Duel! Duel!'

"But then out of the BMW came a second man, on the heels of Bennani. And what a man he was! He was a hulk. Huge. Mean. He rolled his large shoulders proudly, showed off a strangler's hands, and his square jaw quivered menacingly. He was dressed in black and wearing glasses of the same color. *Black!*"

"The detail!"

"Out of instinct, we bookworms huddled before the door of the party hall on the Avenue des Forces-Armées-Royales, we bookworms, out of instinct, take a step back. Murmurs of astonishment. ('Who is this guy?' '*Chkoune hadak?*' '*Mnin khrouj dak James Bond?*') Bennani, seeing that the door of the party hall was closed (that imbecile Mourtada had not yet returned), leans against the wall, calm, and lights a John Player Special—he would never have been caught raising a Casa Sports to his lips. Dadouche, vexed (his attempt to defy Bennani by gaze had been stopped short), demands:

"'Hey, Bennani, who is this guy?'

"Wisps of smoke hovering below his nostrils, Bennani responds, as if stating the obvious:

"'He's my bodyguard.'

"And bam! Knocked back down, our ridiculous clothes, our cologne *made in España,* our shoes polished with Kiwi. As usual, the rich had distanced us by choosing another arena. (The rich shift the debate: that's their great strength. They are always where we don't expect them.) Distressed, we looked at the bodyguard with bulging eyes—we had never seen one from so close up. His face looked the part, and his gestures even more so. He positioned himself between us and his master and banged his right fist against his left hand. We were submerged in our astonishment. Zriwil asked:

"'Your...what?'

"The bodyguard set about examining us all from up close, starting with Zriwil.

"'One wrong word and I'll kill you...'

"'What, wrong word? All of our words are in bad shape, busted, broken...It was only yesterday that we were introduced to Hugo. And plus, we're friends with Bennani,' replied Dadouche.

"Meanwhile, Mourtada had returned, with the stride of a melancholic ferret, and we were able to enter into the party hall. Some sandwiches were moping in a corner, next to some withering drinks. A big banner, stretched across the width of the room, proclaimed the pride of the bus drivers to finally have their union. Yellow garlands trickled from the ceiling, looking like they'd hung themselves the day after the party. The boss, who had spared no expense, had installed an old Teppaz survived from the Titanic and exactly three records: Aznavour, *Petite musique de nuit,* and Nana Mouskouri (*Greatest Hits*). We were over the moon (*c'était Byzance*) but not Bennani. He threw down the covers with a disdainful air after barely looking at them.

"'What is this junk shop?'

"That was how he crushed us, routinely. If someone was excited, he would denigrate: he had seen better, he knew better. Better: he *possessed* better. What am I saying? *He was better.*

"He shrugged his shoulders.

"'I'll bring you real music,' he decides.

"He leaves, followed by his bodyguard, to rummage through the trunk of the BMW and comes back, followed by his body-guard, with a big cardboard box, and in a flick of the wrist, LPs galore. Marvin Gaye, Paul Anka, the Supremes…Through this room barely widowed of its unionists echoes the animal desire glorified by soul music:

"*Let's get it on…*

"Bennani grooves a bit, is imitated by his bodyguard, closes his eyes, then says:

"'This song is magic, girls drop like flies listening to it, if you had brought your chicks…'

"The phrase lingers, unanswered. We lower our heads, mortified. As for 'chicks,' we had among us only three little bookworms, Najla and two others, our classmates, who bore the brunt of our fantasies but who seemed to be interested only in math—not in us, with our faces looking like we'd been dug up from the grave.

"The night unfolds normally, which is to say abnormally: three girls, sixty starving people—and Marvin Gaye. Standing in a corner, smoking his John Player Specials, Bennani observes us: he's at the zoo. His bodyguard, who plays with a nonexistent earpiece, drinks beer after beer: it's free, because who would dare ask for money from such a massive guy? From time to time, he inspects."

"Inspects what?"

"Well, everything…he taps on the walls, like you do when you search for a hollow, with the palm of his left hand flat and little sudden knocks with the bent index finger of the other hand… He stares defiantly at the banner of the unionists. He sizes up the sandwiches, relieves them, if necessary, of their garniture (mortadella can be quite dangerous). He opens the door and examines the Avenue des Forces-Armées-Royales, so propitious to the rise of tanks. He comes to look at us from up close, with a suspicious air, as if we were cooking up an assassination attempt. He purports even to frisk the body of the little Najla, who escapes by screeching. He asks for identification from the landlord, who had come to check that everything was going okay. The landlord takes offense (he is after all in his own place), we nearly have an incident, the bodyguard has to rein himself in.

"So much so that we begin to feel sorry for him, this man with nothing to do. Ahmidouch asks him where he's from. 'Settat!' he responds, as others might say New York or Paris. We look at each other, astonished—there's a school for bodyguards at Settat? He misunderstands our hesitation. Menacingly:

"'Do you have a problem with that?'

"Not at all, we explain to him. And the accusing index fingers are extended: he's from Benahmed, him (the fat one) from Tata, him from Sefrou, him (the little guy) from Sidi-Bennour, I'm from Fkih Ben Salah…

"The strongman of Halles can't believe it. He thought we were all sons of the upper class, bourgeois, loaded, from Casablanca or maybe even from Fes…And he finds out we're as much of a bumpkin as he is! Dumbstruck (I've been wanting to say that for a while now), he goes to check that the avenue hasn't changed directions. Then he comes back, as if some dawn is beginning to glow beneath his neurons. He murmurs:

"'But you're all sons of the masses…'

"A collective shudder courses through us. You have to remember that this story takes place in an age when three people out of two were part of the police, where snitches abounded, where you could be denounced by your own shadow—the bitch. Expressions like 'sons of the masses' that seem harmless today rang out at the time like a proclamation along the lines of: 'I am Marxist-Leninist and I plan to overthrow the government.'

"In any case, the fact that Mr. Bodyguard used such a dangerous expression suggested to us that: 1) he was crazy; 2) he was a snitch; 3) he was drunk. The truth was probably a combination of the three (1+2+3).

"As soon as the words are heard and their dangerousness percolates in our brains, we disperse throughout the party hall, not wanting to finish the year in prison—we had competitions and exams to worry about. The bawdyguard follows us (he divides in two, in three, in umpteen), clinging to some of us, embracing others, smooching Najla and proclaiming urbi et 'roubi, to the city and to us country folk, that he loves us all, on the whole and in the details. Bennani, standing in a corner, stunned, was like Napoleon looking on as Moscow burned, with no fire extinguisher.

"His bodyguard is crying now, so sloshed from the alcohol we could have set him ablaze with a snap of the fingers. He stammers, snot deforming his words:

"'You are all sons of the masses…Like me.'

"He turns, by chance, toward the native of Sidi-Bennour.

"'My name is Bouchta! And you, my brother, what did God name you?'

"'Jilali,' the Sidi-Bennourien affirms proudly.

"The bodyguard steps back a few centimeters and stares at Jilali's pants. They're pants that (how can I phrase it?)…have lived. They were originally corduroy, probably. A long time ago. Then, at the mercy of rubbing against the back of CTM bus seats (the most cramped in the world, calibrated for Pinocchio); of the abrasion suffered from rough chairs; against entryways waiting for a door to open; on the sidewalk, the days of lining up in front of the police station, waiting for the forces of Law and Order to hand over an identity card; against the trees on the boulevard; the stadium bleachers; the deteriorated, discouraged walls; on the asphalt, if there was a fight or skirmish…at the mercy of all that, the corduroy was no longer ribbed and barely corded; now it looked like one of those humble fabrics we turn into dish towels—and these were Jilali's Sunday pants.

"The bodyguard turns toward another guy.

"'And you,' he asks the Fkih Ben Salah native, 'what name did

God give you?'

"'Cherki,' replies Cherki.

Bouchta the bodyguard attentively examines the aforementioned shirt of Cherki. It has traveled, it's undeniable. One can speculate it's had an adventurous life, come from a weaving loom from the age of the Hittites, falling cleanly on Assyrian buttocks, at the beginning, then little by little deteriorating, passed from one person to another in the great movement of migrations toward the West, debarking one day from a dhow or a felucca, along with a thousand of its sisters, prisoner of privateers, thrown in a heap on the floor of illegal souks, grabbed by a speculator who puts it up in a dark alley the next day to sell for a profit ("It's from Germany, my brother!"), and it's Cherki who acquires it, moved, dreaming of the effect that beautiful shirt, only the tiniest bit worn, will have on the little Najla when he sports it at the big party where he finds himself presently, the eye of the bodyguard fixed on him. The bodyguard intensifies his sobs while his retinas dart back and forth between Cherki's rag and Bennani's shirt, designed by a Parisian couturier, brought from Paris by the arrogant Airbus, unwrapped the same morning as it had been packaged in silk paper by a maid with eyes lowered, pressed (the shirt) even if it was of no use. Bouchta repeats, tearful:

"'You are all sons of the masses…Like me.'

"Bennani, understanding that everything was going to heck in a handbasket, wrests himself from his promontory and comes to take the human rag by the arm to drag him toward the light of the avenues. But nothing could be done: the man frees himself in one move, seizes his master by the throat and yells out:

"'But you! You! You are not a son of the masses!'

"Shock! The masks fall. The troupe fraternizes. Comrades, drop your weapons! Marvin Gaye stops singing: the promise of a happier tomorrow. *El pueblo, unido*...The banner flaps in the wind—now it's taking on all its meaning—the meaning of History. The owner of the hall has disappeared: he probably went to go alert the police. We other bookworms, we watch the scene, eyes bulging. So many things happening! The garde du corps bellows in the face of Bennani before him, spraying him copiously with spit and with his class hatred, and hurls out:

"'I'm gonna kill you!'

"Bennani runs away, his hands awkwardly hanging onto the lapels of his jacket, like a diligent turkey; he breaks through the door and runs toward the BMW. The bodyguard follows him, light-footed Achilles, with us on his heels. The rest, the murder, the decisive blow, happens in the blink of an eye. Pif, paf...Hissing of the noble fabric of his shirt...Crack of the collector's item watch smashing on the cobblestone...Bennani lies on the sidewalk, nose smashed, writhing in pain. The bodyguard retreats into the night with a supple step, head sunken into his shoulders. He's stopped crying, only his haughty sniffling recalls the outbursts from earlier. He turns around and from a distance yells to us in a manly voice, no longer trembling:

"'Adieu, boys! Bouchta salutes you!'

"Indeed, he said 'Bouchta.'

"He was no longer 'the bodyguard' of anybody.

"He was a free man."

THE INVENTION OF DRY SWIMMING

At Café de l'Univers, there were six of us, seated, observing the comings and goings of our Casablancan citizens, during a lovely lethargic afternoon in the month of May; but it could have been another place, another day, different people. It could have been Tunisia, April, a crisp morning. Seoul, December, night, all of us lying down. On the other hand, what Hamid told us was truly incredible and unique. He hadn't said a word for an hour. Taciturn, meditating. Lost in the labyrinth of his neurons. A guy had asked us the way to the cathedral, which had brought about biblical complications. When the dust had settled again and the man had left, Hamid finally shook himself, opened his mouth, and started to talk. He began with a loose characterization of Moroccans:

"We are," said Hamid (he paused), "we are (he swallowed a sip of coffee), we are (he put down his cup) an inventive people."

He had put the word in italics. So we examined it closely. Then we demanded, silent, the proof (we, too, know how to use italics). Confronted with this nonverbal wall, this walled-in wall, Hamid had no other alternative than to elaborate.

"I say this because, while you were grappling with that persistent man, I remembered a curious affair that took place in the '70s near El Jadida. It was all about, or rather it all started

94

with, a memorandum from the Minister of National Education, a memorandum coated in the pompous style we affected in those days—and in classical Arabic if you please, the language of Jahiz and Mutanabbi. This memorandum arrived one day, like a swirling dead leaf, on the desk of all the leaders of the establishment…"

"They all shared one desk?"

Hamid, shrugging his shoulders, ignored Khalid's interruption.

"…a memorandum informing them that a new discipline had been registered in the program for the sports portion of the baccalaureate: swimming!"

A sip of coffee, inhaled noisily, punctuated this revelation that we sensed was heavy with consequences—but which exactly? Had water in a cage, in cubic meters, ever threatened anyone? (Heavy water, maybe?) Chlorine poisoning? Stings from stray jellyfish? Amoebas? We digressed in aquatic conjectures. Hamid, his molecule of java ingested, continued his story:

"The memorandum concluded thus, threatening: all necessary measures must be taken so that those among the candidates who choose this discipline for the baccalaureate, this new discipline, can do so in the best conditions. With my most sincere regards, etc., etc. Signed: the Minister of National Education. Followed (I imagine) by a moment of astonishment. Then the leaders of the establishment held their heads in their hands…"

"…in their one office?"

"…held their heads in their hands (at least, I assume, because I wasn't there), and a single roar ascended into the untroubled azure of the peaceful El Jadida skies: WHAT?"

Ali felt impelled to contribute his grain of salt to the affair.

He protested:

"Hang on! It would amaze me if we were able to roar the word 'what,' which is, by the way, a pronoun. At best we might cackle or caw pronouncing it."

Jamal:

"Or squeal it. We can squeal 'what.'"

Hamid shook his head.

"Imbeciles. We can roar all the words of the dictionary. We can snarl them, bray them. It's all in the intonation, the timbre, the breath."

"Tra-la-la, pee-pee, hip-hop—there are plenty of words we can't roar. Let alone snarl or bray."

Nagib snapped his fingers, as if he had resolved a particularly difficult enigma.

"I understand now why lions have such a limited vocabulary: they can roar essentially nothing. That said, I don't really know when a lion would have the opportunity to use tra-la-la, pee-pee, or hip-hop in a conversation. At night, in the savannah."

Hamid put an end to these flights of fancy by loudly striking the table.

"Shut up, all of you! This is my story, let me tell it or I'll keep quiet and never open my mouth again!"

"Oh my...Look how mad he's getting...Go on, tell us, tell us."

Hamid started up his story again:

"If the leaders of the establishment took their heads in their hands as one man, if they roared WHAT? as one wild beast, it was because they had immediately seen the problem, ze big problem, which was..."

He interrupted himself to bend down and pet the cat, leaving us to simmer in our curiosity. Then he straightened up and began again, his voice cavernous, his eyes tragic, index finger raised as if he were at last revealing the third secret of Fatima:

"…which was the regrettable, deplorable, but nevertheless irrefutable, absence of even the smallest swimming pool in El Jadida!"

Boom! So that was it. We got down to brass tacks concerning the tragedy, the complications, the eleventh dimension. He leaned toward us all, which was a bit of a feat since there were five of us (excluding him), necessitating that he contort himself into the barycenter of a hexagon:

"Nothing! Zilch! No pool! Nada (you can say that again)!"

Nagib furrowed his brow:

"But wait a minute…I vaguely remember those days, I was a kid then, but…Wasn't there a pool at the campsite run by Madame Muñoz's husband? I mean her second husband, the Moroccan, what was his name?"

Time stood still as all six of us tried to remember what the devil the name of Madame Muñoz's (Moroccan) husband was.

"Tarik? Abdelmoula? El Haj? Abdallah? Maati? Miloud? Robio? Driss? Lgouchi? Bouazza? Mohamed? El Ghoul Jr.? Hassan?"

A quarter of an hour went by before we all agreed that we had never known the name of Madame Muñoz's (Moroccan) husband. We saw him sometimes in her villa; he would water the garden, play with the dog, smoke a cigarette, go in, go out…He was an anonymous type, it seemed, or if he had a name, he never revealed it to us, for his entire essence came down to the fact that he was the (Moroccan) husband of Madame Muñoz, and that sufficed for a name, like all men who merge with an exploit—the man who saw a bear, the man who beat El Gourch in a bicycle race, etc. For Madame Muñoz was beautiful and rich, like all French women, and so tell me how a little guy from El Jadida had managed to replace—in her heart and in her bed—her first husband, who was French and thus handsome and rich? It was an exploit at least as worthy of being recognized as that of the man who beat El Gourch (in a bicycle race).

"Anonymous or not," resumed Nagib, "that guy managed the campsite, didn't he? And there was a pool in the campsite, wasn't there?"

"Yes and no," responded Ali.

"What do you mean, yes and no? What kind of logic is that?"

"There was a pool, in the guides and on the sign at the city entrance; there was one in rumor, in hearsay, and in memory. But there wasn't one on the site, where it should have been: it had been filled in by the previous managers, the Révolles, who had had a lot of children and who worried that one of them would fall in."

"But it was still, nevertheless, indicated on the sign?"

"The tourists, once they were stationed on the campsite, once they had slipped into their swimsuits and let out a cry of joy (in anticipation), searching in vain for a pool in which to cool down, were angry and disappointed, but never mind, Madame Muñoz's (Moroccan) husband showed them the way to the beach, immense and empty, and they went en masse to drown themselves in the Atlantic."

Hamid, glacial, murmured:

"Are we done now? Can we forget about the untitled husband

of mother Muñoz? Can we forget about the Révolles and their non-regulatory campsite? Can I continue?"

"Yeah, yeah, no, no, go on."

"So: the absence of even the least swimming pool in El Jadida. Whence the problem (at the time, we used the word 'problem' and not 'concern' as we do now), whence the problem: how were they to obey the memorandum from Rabat? Then Hammou, the director of the Abou-Chouaïb-Doukkali High School, had a genius idea. After despairing for an entire day, like all of his colleagues, after envisaging resignation, failure to comply, alcohol, he took the letter from Rabat back to his office, bringing the memorandum up close to his eye—the good one—scrutinizing it closely, and then (I imagine) a smile lit up his pirate face, his eye twinkled and he said: hehe!"

"An eloquent man."

"Hehe, he repeated, unable to shout 'eureka!' Hehe, he repeated; for he had noticed a detail that changed everything: the memorandum from the minister mentioned swimming, but did not specify swimming in water."

Intense excitement at Café de l'Univers. We looked at each other, taken aback. After a few moments of floundering, so to speak, Ali summed up our stupefaction:

"Swimming in water... You know of other kinds?"

Hamid very slowly nodded his head, his eyes expressionless, his breath barely perceptible, like a tortoise that knows something you don't. He cleared his throat and demanded, Socratically:

"What is swimming, deep down?"

"Exactly, it mustn't take place deep down," replied Nagib. "One must remain on the surface."

"You big idiot! When I ask 'What is swimming?' I'm being rhetorical. I'm not waiting for someone to answer me, I'll answer myself. And my answer is this: swimming is, above all, movements. Movements! Yes, messieurs! That's why we say swimming strokes."

Hamid lifted himself halfway up on his seat and seemed to convulse. Worried, we looked for the Moor, so that he might quickly fetch a doctor, or, if unable to find one, the corner healer, with his herbs and dried lizards. Then we understood that Hamid was in fact in the middle of essplanining something, like the philosopher who proves his theories by acting them out, Hamid was demonstrating swimming by swimming in the ("golden brown") air of Casablanca.

"The art of the swimmer," he said, gesticulating furiously, "lies in stringing together the appropriate movements. The chest, the legs, the arms—all move in a coordinated fashion. Harmoniously. It's the crux of the affair: there are only gestures. Propulsion? Well, propulsion is nothing, my friends. It follows naturally."

We considered this proposition for a moment. Ali triggered the counterattack.

"Wait… If propulsion follows naturally, if, in other words, it is only secondary to the swimmer's art, why is it that competitions are decided in the order in which the athletes arrive at their destination? The fastest wins; thus, propulsion is the most important thing."

"False. It is scientifically proven that it's the quality of the movements that assures propulsion: thus it merely follows naturally. Look at the bumpkins bobbing on Sundays at Sidi Bouzid.

Most of them 'doggy paddle,' which consists by and large of doing a lot of uncoordinated movements, as long as they manage to keep their heads above the water. These bumpkins don't move more than a centimeter. You can continue your conversation with them, you on the beach, them in the water; after a quarter of an hour, they're still there, wriggling and telling you about the moussem of Moulay Abdallah. While the rare person who manages to imitate the crawl, or the breaststroke, well, they manage in the end to travel a bit. I repeat: swimming is, above all, movements."

We were not convinced.

"Alright, we're convinced. So?"

"So, Hammou, the director of Abou-Chouaïb-Doukkali high school, decided to organize the swimming exams in the high school playground. Not in the water, because there was none, but on the sand."

This gave rise to one single shout at Café de l'Univers:

"WHAT?"

Hamid, imperturbable:

"Indeed! Sand! All they needed was to bring in a sufficient quantity and place it in the playground in a big regulatory rectangle: twenty by six meters. And the wheels were set in motion! Well, I suppose 'The wheels were stuck in sand!' would be a more accurate metaphor."

We were blown away.

"That's crazy! We don't remember this story at all. Are you sure this happened in El Jadida? Are you sure you didn't make it up?"

"It is perfectly authentic. It was before your time."

"Oh okay, alright, fine, okay."

"So Hammou calls his colleagues and tells them to meet him in a café next to the local public theater, the one that's falling to ruin today but which had its hour of glory. My father saw Jacques Brel sing there…"

"Can you 'see' someone sing? Wouldn't you say my father heard Jacques Brel sing there?"

"Are you calling my father blind? He paid his five dirhams, he was in the second row behind the Corcos, the governor, and Madame Dufour, and he saw, with his eyes, Jacques Brel sing. But why are you trying to p…me off with Jacques Brel? I was talking about the café that was next to the local theater…"

Ali interrupts:

"Ah yes! It was called La Marquise or La Duchesse or some similar nonsense but everyone called it Dadouchi's since the owner was named Dadouchi. Incidentally, even after his death, we still called it Dadouchi's even though someone named Bouchta took over the café, which was officially called La Marquise or La Duchesse—but we continued to say Dadouchi's—which was rather macabre seeing as the guy was lying in the local cemetery."

"Bizarre. We referred to this place with a name that had nothing to do with its owner? Isn't there a philosophical problem there?"

Hamid stood up and pretended to take off.

"Alright, well if my story doesn't interest you…"

"No, no, stay. We won't say another word."

Hamid grumbled, for appearances, shooed the cat and sat back down.

"So, Hammou explained his idea to his colleagues at Dadouchi's. Everyone found the idea ingenious. They congratulate him, they promise him a blowout kefta grill, they marry his daughter on the spot. Everyone's happy. Everyone, except one person: the director of the Ibn-Khaldoun high school, a certain Tijani. Tijani had a problem, let's say a problem of luxury: a beautiful lawn, a legacy of the Protectorate, decorated the playground of his establishment. He was very proud of it and looked after it with the meticulousness of an Englishman, manicure scissors, sprinkler on standby. Out of the question, he roared right in the middle of La Princesse (that's what Dadouchi's café was called, not La Marquise or La Duchesse as Ali claims), out of the question, he roared, to dump cartloads of sand on that marvel which constituted more or less the only green space in the city! His colleagues shrugged their shoulders. He persisted: we'll do without quartz and silica! 'And how will you accomplish this miracle?' mocked his colleagues, who had already forgotten that swimming in sand was also not very common—how quickly we adapt. 'You'll see!' he replied, mysterious. And he leaves them there in La Princesse, astonished. The next day, first thing in the morning, he asks one of his students, rather supple, rather soft (so as not to ruin anything, you'll understand in a minute), he asks him to try to swim on the lawn. The student doesn't understand: why this harassment? He wasn't any rowdier than the others. Tijani essplains to him that it's not a punishment, but an ultra secret project. Is NASA involved? the student asks. Or maybe the CIA? Tijani pushes him down onto the grass; the student contorts, pants, and moves, oh miracle; proving thus that it was doable, as the director had thought, now rubbing his hands together excitedly while the earthworm continued to crawl. That very night, at the café adjoining the local theater, which was called (I remember now) La Royale, and not La Princesse, that very night, Tijani announces to his colleagues that his students would train on the green grass, the gift from God."

"Why 'gift from God'? Sand was created by God, too."

"Okay but stop right there, you're not going to compare sand and grass?"

"Why not?"

"But…grass, it's green, it's vibrant, it synthesizes I don't know what exactly, and it drinks water, I mean, s…it's different from inert, stupid sand, which results from the degradation of rock."

"Certainly. But everything is divine creation, isn't it? So why rhapsodize and roar 'oh, the great gift of God!' when faced with a waterfall, a beautiful tree, or a cloud, and say nothing when staring at a pebble or listening to a braying donkey?"

"I repeat: because sand results from degradation of granite and other rocks. For God creates, He doesn't degrade. That's perhaps the work of the Devil or at least of Nature, which doesn't deserve any better, the villain. While vegetation is the exact opposite of degradation, of putrefaction…"

(You'll see, he's going to talk to us about "dissipative structures.")

"…it's like dissipative structures…"

(See?)

"…they introduce order within disorder. After all, we can't treat as equal that which makes a mess of things and that which picks up after itself."

"In other words, God only created that which is beautiful and orderly? Who created the ugly, the disorderly, the dumps?"

"The Devil, probably."

"You're lucky it's hot out today, otherwise I wouldn't let this load of nonsense slide."

Hamid waited patiently for the theological storm to pass and then continued his story as if nothing had happened:

"Then Tijani announces, standing up, as if towering over the stupefied La Royale, that his students, you see, will be taking the bac swimming test on the grass; it is out of the question for him to transform into a miniature Sahara his lovely lawn, inaugurated in its time by Marshall Lyautey (go ahead and try to prove him wrong). Silence in the ranks of La Royale. The other leaders of the establishment furrow their brows, make eye contact—was there a reason to complain, to oppose him? No, they decide, and they order: who wants a coffee, who wants a beer? Then Hammou stands up. Stop right there! He is not having it. What is this bunk? Standing opposite Tijani—like two cowboys at the end of a film—he formulates what I propose we refer to henceforth as Hammou's Theorem: 'It is easier to swim on grass than on sand.' The statement rings out in La Royale like the conclusion of a scientific presentation, just before the thunder of applause. Someone ventures: 'Are you sure?' Hammou stands by it: 'It is easier to swim on grass than on sand!' The bac candidates at Tijani's school will be at an advantage compared to the others. This was unacceptable! The exclamation point was worth a veto."

"The plot thickens."

"The polemic splinters instantly. La Royale divides into two camps: on the port side, those who accept Hammou's Theorem. Starboard, those who refute it a priori—we are not yet at the proofs. The arguments are flung into the air like gyrfalcons flying out of their native ossuary. Those pro-Hammou cite the viscosity of the blades of grass and the morning dew; those pro-Tijani counter with the rollability of grains of sand. Finally, the doyen of the leaders of the establishment…"

"Who? Zerhouni?"

"…finds the solution: call in a specialist of fluid mechanics. Abdeljebbar, his nephew, was an engineer who graduated from the École Mohammedia for engineers and, as such, knew the Navier-Stokes equations, which determine, as you are aware, fluid mechanics. They called in Abdeljebbar, who lived five minutes away. He came. Was informed of the problem. Squinted his eyes. Pouted. Took a notebook out of his pocket. Etched a few very elegant curves. And decided thus: the results obtained for swimming on sand must be multiplied by a factor of 1.2 to be compared to those obtained on grass. Still all that depends on the quality of sand and on the ambient hygrometry, but anyway, if we kept track of all the variables and of all the parameters needed to resolve a problem, we would still be in the stone ages."

"Problem solved."

"Not quite. The head of the establishment of Lalla Zahra, a certain Zniga, entered the scene. Possessing neither sand nor grass, Zniga proposed adding gravel into the list of water substitutes. It was too late, since everyone had accepted sand, grass, and the coefficient 1.2."

"Gravel? That's not a sport anymore, it's torture."

"That's what La Royale unanimously decided: Zniga was denounced. (As an aside: this was perhaps the day that began Zniga's decline. 'Denounced by his peers,' as wrote the local correspondent of *Le Matin*, he shut himself away in morose silence, which degenerated into a sort of nervous breakdown and he ended up assassinating two attorneys a few years later. But anyway, that's another story.) So all the high school students of El Jadida began to prepare for this strange swimming test that promised surprises, perhaps even world records—in slowness, naturally, but that's still something. The day of, everything went well. Diving was out of the question, of course. Some jumped in the sand, others stepped over a small fence and found themselves grasping at grass."

"Which is better than finding yourself grasping at straws."

"…they set about swimming diligently and, at the end of the day and taking into account the 1.2 coefficient imposed by Abdeljebbar, everyone had their grade."

"All's well that ends well."

"Almost. For there was the case of Talal. Do you remember Talal? Whom we nicknamed Bouboule, because he was really fat? Talal was a boy with no story, with no collective importance, barely an individual. His mother was invisible, his brothers insignificant, his sisters nonexistent, his cat scared. His father wasn't much of anything, some kind of clerk in a trial court or something of that sort, or perhaps not, perhaps he only gave off the air of running through court hallways, busy, rushed, jabot utterly askew, like those men who call themselves doctors for twenty years and then one day it comes to light that they can't read or write. But this clerk, real or illusory, Talal's father, kept in his wallet a document of the highest importance. Guess what it was, friends?"

"A map of Treasure Island?"

"The blueprint for the atomic bomb?"

"The list?"

"No, you band of donkeys. (What list?) What he guarded preciously in his wallet was a rectangle of a few centimeters in length: a business card. But careful! Not just any business card! It was…"

He withdrew into his chair and subsumed us in a gaze sparkling with commiseration (for we didn't know).

"It was the business card of the king's chef!"

General commotion.

"Don't forget that this story takes place at the beginning of the '70s. Everything related, closely or distantly, to the Palace made the masses tremble with fear. The man who buttons up Hassan II's shirt cuffs has more power than a minister. He who shines his boots commands generals. So, his chef! I don't know how the evanescent clerk procured that business card but he hinted that the king's head butler was a cousin of his and, as a result, this calling card that he only exhibited on rare occasions conferred on him an infinite prestige. You didn't mess around with Talal's father."

"Precisely, let's get back to Talal…"

"I'm getting there. So, the young Talal jumps in the sand, spreads out over it like an obese tarantula, swims haphazardly, but—catastrophe!—he faints a few meters from the rope that symbolizes the edge of the pool. Sunburn? Exhaustion? Abulia? No one knows. His classmates, on solid ground, cry out, wave him on, encourage him…Nothing works, he looks like a recumbent marble statue petrified by a gust of wind. Talal lies still. Talal doesn't move. His professor, a bit of a risk-taker, throws himself into the sand and fishes out the poor boy. There he is in the middle of the playground, awoken by a few vigorous slaps. 'Where am I, who am

I, etc.'. That night, at home, he rests, surrounded by the affection
of his invisible mother, of his insignificant brothers, of his nonexistent sisters, and of his cat that scrams, frightened. His father
enters and announces to him coldly that he received a zero in the
swimming test. General affliction, the ghosts groan, insignificance
clenches its fists, the feline redoubles its pusillanimity. But what
could be done? Spurred on by his pater (who fondles the business
card in his pocket), Talal goes to the high school the next day and
drops off a complaint. In essence, it said, conditionals included:
'If I had taken the swimming test in water, as do civilized people,
and not in sand, I would not have washed up flailing on the aforementioned sand and thus would not have failed the test'—which,
I mention in passing, was formulated with a rare grammatical
accuracy. 'You would not have washed up, nitwit,' replied his
professor. 'You would have sunk like a stone and you would be
dead.' And he adds, digressing, as professors often do: 'By the way,
a mammal cannot wash up on sand.'"

Nagib is outraged:

"He's wrong. Whales wash up on sand. Whales are mammals."

"No, they're fish."

(Thus ensues a pointless discussion, which has taken place in all
ages and all latitudes, on what whales are—meanwhile people are
dying of hunger (in their case, a whale, conveniently carved up,
would be most welcome [but are they halal?]. Victory to Nagib
and all of science: cetaceans are mammals. End of digression.)

"Anyway, the affair reaches the head of the establishment. It's
true that Talal had not finished the race…"

"He finished it on the sand," Nagib intervenes.

"But he had begun it on the sand," Ali retorts. "At what point do these millions of grains cease to be sand and become a part of the fiction?"

Hamid shrugs his shoulders and continues his story.

"The leader of the establishment thinks of the clerk's business card. He knows he's in a minefield. Talal did not finish the race but there is perhaps a way to come to an agreement. He decides then to give a grade to the toothed whale in proportion to his breaching…"

"Breaching?"

"It's the technical term. The breaching becomes thus a relative failure. Since Talal traveled two thirds of the pool, or rather the dry dock, he would have the same grade as one of his classmates who was at his distance at the time of his wreck (if I dare say it)—a grade lowered, however, by a third to take into account the fact that he did not faint in the middle of his efforts. I said we were an inventive people. And that's how the whole affair came to end."

Hamid had said it. He had even proved his starting assertion. At Café de l'Univers, all six of us remained for a long moment in silence, in that lovely unending afternoon. I don't know what my friends or the cat were thinking about. I was seized by a strong emotion—tears came to my eyes, my heart tightened. It was gone forever, that blessed age, where we faced, imperturbable, the most absurd problems fate thrust upon us. I closed my eyes…I saw once more those faces of El Jadida: the governor, enigmatic; the super, attendant; Madame Corcos, who led the majorettes on the boulevard once a year; Charef the sworn interpreter, who was originally from Algeria (we forgave him); the doctor Argyatos;

the owner of the Bata boutique; the local correspondent for
Le Matin. We were a city proud of its Portuguese past and its hybrid
present. We were unsure of nothing, capable of anything—even of
inventing dry swimming. But where are the sands of days gone by?

FIFTEEN MINUTES AS PHILOSOPHERS

The classroom door opens. Amir and Sylvie enter, a bit intimidated. They take a few steps, look at the walls, the board, the tables…

AMIR (*murmurs*)
Well, here I am… *here we are* back in our old classroom…Here where you taught your philosophy class…

SYLVIE (*she interrupts him*)
Was it really this room? Are you sure?

AMIR (*looks around then shrugs his shoulders*)
This one or another one…They all look the same, after all.

SYLVIE (*she paces back and forth while Amir takes a seat and looks at her*)
No, not really. Personally, I liked the rooms where they taught geography. The colored maps on the wall, the globe on the desk… what a dream. Although…Today's maps don't have any more white zones, unexplored territories or places where no one has ever set foot. In antiquity, the maps of Africa had only one indication: *hic sunt leones*. (*She laughs.*) "Here, there are lions!" But there are no more lions in Morocco, unfortunately. The last was captured in 1912… (*She turns back toward Amir.*) Why are you smiling?

AMIR (*still smiling*)

Because here you are once again starting on a long monologue…
Digressions…Like before. Incidentally, we used to call you "the
overflowing river" more often than "Madame Rivière, the philosophy professor."

SYLVIE

"Mademoiselle," please. I wasn't married.

AMIR

Yes, but we called you *Madame* Rivière. (*He makes an offhand
gesture with his hand.*) Madame, mademoiselle…We didn't make
the distinction.

SYLVIE (*daydreaming*)

Believe me, there is one. (*She laughs nervously.*) I felt it happen…
Ahem! (*She pulls herself together.*) I say, "the overflowing river," that
wasn't very nice. I had just arrived from France, I was barely twenty-
five years old, I wanted to teach you everything. You seemed
like fledglings eagerly awaiting their beak…Well, not everyone…
There were of course the loafs in the back…who seemed less
interested in Kant or Bergson than in… (*she crosses her arms across
her chest.*) in, what's the word? My tits? (*She shakes her head.*) The
loafs…I wonder what's become of them. Sociologists, probably.
(*She laughs.*) But the others, I wanted to teach them *everything*.
Thus my *mo-no-logues*, my *di-gres-sions*, as you say. And philosophy…well, philosophy, it encompasses everything, everything is a
part of it! (*Finger raised, sententiously*) Even mathematics is just a
branch of philosophy!

AMIR (*mockingly*)
Mathematics? You know how to solve a differential equation?

SYLVIE
A what?

AMIR
A diff-fer-en-tial e-qua-tion.

SYLVIE
Ha, ha, very funny. Unfortunately, the branches of knowledge split very early on and we can't learn everything. I studied philosophy in the strictest sense of the term.

AMIR (*coldly*)
I couldn't have said it better myself.

SYLVIE (*approaching Amir*)
So it's in a classroom like this one that it happened... What you call your "score to settle." Is that it, the expression you used yesterday?

AMIR
Yes. How to explain? I don't know where to begin. The problem...

SYLVIE (*interrupting him*)
Why do you call it a "problem"?

AMIR
It doesn't matter what we call it! "Problem," "question," "concern," as we've been saying for the past few years. (*Snickering*) "*Souci!*" It's the name of a flower... there's nothing more insipid than that! As if we're afraid of words. Who decided the word "problem"

was too scary and we shouldn't use it anymore? Probably some marketing hotshot...

SYLVIE

Probably one of the dunces from the old days...

TOGETHER:

...now a sociologist! (*She laughs. He snickers.*)

AMIR

Anyway, the problem...Well, you're the one who posed it.

SYLVIE

Me?

AMIR

Yes. Starting with your first philosophy class. That famous Pascal text...I still remember. "When I consider the short duration of my life, swallowed up in the eternity before and after, the little space which I fill, and even can see, engulfed in the infinite immensity of spaces of which I am ignorant, and which know me not, I am frightened, and am astonished at being here rather than there; for there is no reason...The eternal silence of these infinite spaces frightens me."

Sylvie

Yes, it's the most famous passage of *Pensées*. Beautiful, isn't it?

Amir (*starts*)

Beautiful? Beautiful?? Sure, but I was sixteen years old! It was the first time that...that I studied philosophy, that I came into contact with "thought." (*He pronounces the word in a grandiloquent tone.*) For me, what you said, it wasn't *beautiful*, it was the truth…A whole new continent opened up, as if…as if my eyes were opened up, too…

SYLVIE
You're exaggerating!

AMIR (*more and more vehement*)
Not at all! It was your job, to teach philosophy. You came to deliver your class and you left. But for me, it was…it was something else. Thought…Doubt! The anxiety that set in! "The short duration of my life in the infinite immensity of spaces…" I barely had the time to digest that and—wham!—Nietzsche was thrust upon me!

SYLVIE (*mocking*)
Alright then! Nietzsche was thrust upon you! Did it hurt?

AMIR (*shrugs his shoulders*)
Go ahead, make fun of me…

SYLVIE (*conciliatory*)
I'm sorry…But which Nietzsche text are you talking about? I don't remember talking about Nietzsche.

AMIR
You did! That business of eternal recurrence!

SYLVIE
Oh right!

AMIR (*agitated*)
It went something like: "One day, or one night, a demon will wake you and say to you: this life, as you now live it and have lived it,

well, you will have to live it once more, in all its details, even the most minuscule; every joy, every sorrow…every thought and every sigh…in the same succession, from beginning to end. The same inescapable sequence! And then you will have to start over, again and again…Indefinitely!" Such anxiety! That day, I couldn't eat anything. I didn't sleep at all that night!

SYLVIE (*astonished*)
I say! If I had known…You were a very sensitive adolescent, very suggestible.

AMIR
And then that phrase by Pascal (him again!) that you repeated so often: "The last act is bloody…"

SYLVIE (*completes the phrase*)
"…however pleasant the rest of the play is. A little earth is thrown at last upon our head, and that is the end forever."

AMIR
"A little earth is thrown at last upon our head…" That depressed me for life…

SYLVIE
You're exaggerating!

AMIR (*stares at her intensely then shrugs his shoulders*)
It was like a veil, a gray cover that fell over me, that fell over the world. That gray cover went with me everywhere. When I went to France to do my studies, it was there. When I returned, it was waiting for me, even under the sun.

As if I had drunk a poison...

SYLVIE

A poison?

AMIR

Yes. The poison of philosophy...

SYLVIE (*interrupting him*)

Stop right there! You're talking like they do in the countries where philosophy is banned...Because it makes you reflect and reflection is dangerous. Dangerous for the power...It's better that people don't reflect, that they remain naive, attached to dogmas that call for obedience above all. That the slave obeys without asking questions, that's the master's dream. But philosophy comes to throw a wrench in the gears...

AMIR (*interrupting her in turn*)

But it's not about that! You were talking about death all the time. That was the ultimate truth. "Life is nothing but a dream," you said...

SYLVIE (*she interrupts him again*)

That's Calderón de la Barca: "What is life? An illusion, a shadow, a fiction...All of life is nothing but a dream, and dreams are nothing but dreams."

AMIR

I thought: "Might as well die then." But if everything was just going to start over, eternally, thanks Nietzsche, what a nightmare! I was stuck. And Pascal, with his "last bloody act"...I had some difficult months because of you.

SYLVIE (*taken aback*)
Because of me?

AMIR
Yes!

SYLVIE
And that's why you insisted on coming back here yesterday when you recognized me in that little café on the coast? That's why you asked me to meet you here at the high school? (*A pause.*) This score to settle, it was…*it is* with me, then?

AMIR
Yes.

SYLVIE (*laughs nervously*)
If we were in an Agatha Christie book…Should I be worried? (*She looks toward the door.*) Is a *constable* or a *moghazni* coming to arrest me? For causing you distress when you were fifteen years old?

AMIR
No, no…That said, there's some truth to what you said. (*He stares at her.*)

SYLVIE (*uneasy*)
Alright, let's go, you've had your fun, let's go now.

AMIR
No!
(*He leaps toward the door, blocks it with a chair and stands before it,*)

arms crossed.)

SYLVIE

I don't find this funny. (*She walks toward the door.*) Let me through!

AMIR

No!

(*They stare each other down.*)

SYLVIE (*right up against him*)
Let me through!

AMIR

Not a chance!
(*He rummages in his jacket pocket and takes out a black revolver that he holds against Sylvie's head.*)

SYLVIE (*she jumps back and screams*)
You're crazy!

AMIR

Yeah, I'm crazy! Crazy, *fou*, *loco*, *h'meq*…But whose fault is that? I was at peace, I asked nothing of anybody…and then philosophy…that obsession with absurdity…with death, that obsession you stuck me with! (*He threatens her with the revolver.*) Sit down!

(*Sylvie goes to sit down on a bench.*)

AMIR

No! Over there! (*He points to the teacher's desk. She sits down.*) And now, to work! You're going to bring me back to how I was before I met you…Carefree! Simple. "Stupid," if you will. Like all the people who don't worry themselves about philosophy, who peacefully believe in God or in Providence, who aren't obsessed with death, nor by what comes after! (*She remains silent.*) Go on! Speak! Now we're going to finish the class. We're going to unravel it all. Make me stupid again! I want to be stupid!

SYLVIE (*sarcastic*)
You're already crazy, that's a start.

AMIR
Ha ha, very funny. But what is madness, anyway? Here we have a subject for philosophy. Come on, let's begin. (*He threatens her with the revolver.*) Go on! Make me stupid again! Rid me of this obsession with death. (*He shouts.*) Go on!

SYLVIE (*frightened*)
Alright. (*Hesitant*) But you're wrong about everything. Certainly, "Philosophy is learning how to die…"

AMIR (*interrupts her, irritated*)
No, that I already know. I don't want to learn how to die, I want to become a child again. Or an idiot. Or both. I want to go back to the time before philosophy. My parents, my family, everyone in this country—they do a few prayers every day, they fast when necessary, give a small coin to a passing beggar—and as a result, they're serene and at peace. They'll go to Paradise, they're sure of it. As for me, I *am* in Hell. Every day! Because of philosophy.

SYLVIE (*furious*)

But that's idiotic! It's exactly the opposite. Philosophy teaches you how to live by teaching you how to die: the two go together. "We who perhaps one day shall die, proclaim man as immortal at the flaming heart of the instant." It's clear, isn't it? (*Amir shakes his head*.) "We who perhaps one day shall die, proclaim man as immortal at the flaming heart of the instant." It's Saint-John Perse…

AMIR

Continue.

SYLVIE

Epicurus said it well. Something like: "I cannot fear death for as long as I am here, it is not here. And when it will be here, I will no longer be here. *Thus*, I will never meet death. *Thus*, I do not need to be afraid of it…"

AMIR

Continue.

SYLVIE

But what more is there to say, after that? Must I keep quoting? "Don't aspire, oh my soul, to immortal life. But exhaust the field of the possible." Pindar said that in 5 B.C. Or else Valéry: "The day is rising, we must try to live!" Or else must I explain yet again the myth of Sisyphus? We must have gone over it in class, no? In any case you know the last words of Camus's essay: "One must imagine Sisyphus happy."

AMIR (*vehemently*)

Yes, but all that, that comes after! After the doubt instilled by philosophy, after the anxiety of death. After the absurd has taken hold in the heart...in the heart of my life, of my existence. I want to return to the innocence of before...before your philosophy class!

SYLVIE
Well, if that's what you want, it's not worth it. There's no going back. One cannot *unlearn*. It's impossible.

AMIR
We can't go back?

SYLVIE
No.

AMIR (*slowly, dully*)
But I could go past anxiety...I could commit myself to a cause bigger than life, bigger than death...Go blow myself up in Iraq or in Afghanistan!

SYLVIE (*sarcastic*)
That's really smart. Give your life out of fear of death! Have you heard about Gribouille? Who takes refuge in a pond to escape the rain?

AMIR (*bursts*)
But then what's left, faced with the anxiety of death?

SYLVIE (*gets up, ardent, makes passionate gestures with outstretched arms*)
But I've just told you! "Proclaim man as immortal at the flaming heart of the instant." Seize the instant! *Carpe diem!* Try to live!

One must imagine Sisyphus happy!

AMIR (*While she's speaking, he slowly raises the gun and brings it to his temple. Sylvie does not notice.*)
Perhaps...But we can also put an end to it right away. It's not worth waiting for the boulder to crash back down. And too bad if it all starts over again.

SYLVIE (*She turns toward him and rushes to stop him from pulling the trigger.*)
No!

AMIR
So long, absurd world!

(*He pulls the trigger. His face is inundated with water. He bursts into laughter and "shoots" at Sylvie. She too is inundated with water.*)

SYLVIE (*furious*)
Imbecile! What is this...this...act?

AMIR (*beaming*)
Life is a dream, the pistol is a water gun. "The whole world are actors." That's Petronius...Sartre said the same thing with his business of *d'en soi et de pour soi*, being-in-itself and being-for-itself. You see, I continued with philosophy, even after.

SYLVIE (*still furious*)
I don't understand. Why all this dramatization?

AMIR (*very calm*)
"Dramatization?" It's precisely that, that's exactly the word!

I dramatized the malaise, the anxiety, into which you plunged me, ten years ago. And now, we're even. The score is settled. I'm dead and so are you. Now we can finally live.

SYLVIE (*She unblocks the door and runs out yelling.*)
Imbecile!

AMIR (*sticks his head out of the small opening of the door*)
Philosopher! Go on then, hey, philosopher! (*He turns toward the audience.*) She never even asked me what I do now.

(A VOICE RISES FROM THE AUDIENCE:)
What do you do now?

AMIR
I'm a philosophy professor, of course!

He takes a deep bow.

THE NIGHT BEFORE

He woke up from a bad sleep, populated with *djinns* and demons, and the first thing he saw, before even being able to murmur "*staghrifoullah*," was a gnome. And this gnome, who resembled his son, was holding in his hands a picket sign imprinted with only one word: *liberty*. The child (or the dwarf?) began to speak—it was strange, he had the voice of an adult. But what was he saying?

"Father...and *my* liberty?"

Why are you calling me father...Omar wanted to ask, vexed, but the words never came: the gnome's face had just undergone the subtlest of transformations—it was and was no longer his son, as if oscillating between two faces, one lost, the other found again. What was the meaning of this mystery? Omar wanted to ask his wife, who had just materialized by the bed—or before him? What was this phenomenon? He saw her in a chiaroscuro, simultaneously from the front and in profile, he saw her as he had never seen her before—but had he ever seen her before? It was as if it were a stranger who was standing there, somewhere, in his living space. Would she dare to breathe? She did better: she apostrophized him. His mouth opened like a canteen. She's apostrophizing me! I'm not even sure what that word means, but that's probably what she's doing—what she's daring to do—and this is probably what they call "the signs of the end of times." The Hour is approaching, the tombs will be dug up, the earth will vomit its entrails... This woman, bestowed upon me by a *fat'ha* in a dark house, dares to speak to me. What is she saying? I'll settle the score with her later. For the moment, let's listen.

"Man, I want to be free."

Where is that damned gnome? Omar lowered his eyes and saw a child watching him, his eyes big, opened wide, as if filled with limpid water. And the child repeated that scandalous word "liberty," then raised his hand and presented his palm to his progenitor: the impious word was displayed on it, etched with ash.

Servant! Maid! Bring me a belt, a bludgeon. I have important business: I must correct wife and child. They address their lord and master without being authorized to do so—did I even summon them? What is this? The start of a debate? I only debate with my peers—I only listen to the *sheikh*—and he only listens to God. That's the sacred chain. If even one link cedes, there's dissent, the thread is broken, the text is unwound. Order keeps the world spinning on its axis, I've been taught that since I was a kid, on the braided mat, in the swaying of bodies through which wave after wave of knowledge enters, raising the walls and erecting the city—where the space belongs to men. Hey, servant! The straps! But what... Here she comes, silent, but voluble in movement, her little fist raised—that limp body can tighten? But this madness is never-ending, but her, too, but... she's brandishing a picket sign. Omar leans in, adjusts an imaginary pair of spectacles and deciphers the consonants forming the word *karama*. Alright then. The maid too? Asking for dignity now... What place does sentiment have here, how is intellect infecting girls, are you something other than exploited at will? Where's the whip? Forget the whip. Bring me a harness. Wife, the harness! It's for the maid, she'll bring me the bludgeon, I'll knock out my disgraceful son—but not before he's brought me the poker. I intend to burn it into your flesh, my wife—but first bring me the harness—I intend to engrave it with a few appropriate sentences—we are not a unique *people* as claim the chess players, but I am the master in my home. Bring me some coal!

And then the world started to spin. They came at him from different angles, sideways, determined—it seemed to him—to shatter the sphere revolving around him. Perhaps this was the moment to propose a truce, an arrangement? He rejected the idea for what it was: the work of the Devil. Besides, it was he who possessed the soul of his son and (if they had them) of his wife and servant. They continued to spin around him, sometimes breaking the circle to draw near his eyes like a flash of lightning, murmuring those words of liberty and dignity that their clumsy fingers had written on the picket signs. He suddenly remembered it was his fingers that had done it. In other words, they had stolen his work! What right did they have? These two women (these two phantoms tormenting me) don't even know how to read—in any case he preferred it that way—which is certainly clear now. But then, the picket signs? Did the troll…? Let's try a diversion. In a brusque movement, Omar seized his wife's wrist, but his fingers closed on empty space, he tried to slap the little servant and met a void, he didn't dare bite his son's neck, afraid of tasting his own blood. My God, will this trial ever come to an end? Why, why did you forget about me…

The despairing man woke up, this time for good. He was covered in sweat. His wife was breathing softly next to him, in a deep sleep. Her regular breathing was barely audible. Outside, the city was humming with the peaceful murmur of a sleeping beauty. So, it had been a bad dream. Curse the Devil! He sat up in his bed, then got up and put on his slippers, preparing to do his ablutions. It was time to give thanks to God.

As he lumbered toward the bathroom, he saw, in the hallway, carefully positioned against the wall, the picket sign he had made the night before. Ah yes, the demonstration, this afternoon…He would be there. Without fail.

WORKS CITED

DISLOCATION

1. "Philosophers have only interpreted the world; the point is to change it."

MARX, KARL. "Theses on Feuerbach." *Karl Marx and Frederick Engels, Selected Works, Volume One.* Trans. W. Lough. Moscow: Progress Publishers, 1969. 13–15.

2. "This one went forth in quest of truth as a hero, and at last got for himself a small decked-up lie: his marriage he calleth it."

NIETZSCHE, FRIEDRICH. *Thus Spake Zarathustra: A Book for All and None.* Trans. Thomas Common. Mineola: Dover Publications, 1999.

3. "The eternal silence of these infinite spaces frightens me."

PASCAL, BLAISE. *Pensées.* Trans. W. F. Trotter. New York: E. P. Dutton & Co., 1958.

4. "To the eyes of the world still intact / It feels grow and weep, unspoken, / Its sharp, underlying crack / Do not touch, it is broken."

PRUDHOMME, SULLY. "Le Vase Brisé." *Stances et Poèmes.* Paris: Alphonse Lemerre, 1866.

Translated by Emma Ramadan.

KHOURIBGA, OR THE LAWS OF THE UNIVERSE

1. "Under the torrents of a tropical sun...which spreads heat over

our fallow lands."
FLAUBERT, GUSTAVE. *Madame Bovary.* Trans. Raymond N. MacKenzie. Indianapolis: Hackett Publishing, 2009.

2. "The spokes of the wheels converge at the hub. They converge toward the empty space. And it's thanks to the empty space that the chariot advances...The vase is made of clay but it's the empty space that makes it a vase."
Paraphrase of Chapter 11 of the *Tao te Ching*, a Chinese classic text attributed to LAO TZU.
Emma Ramadan's translation of Fouad Laroui's French.

FIFTEEN MINUTES AS PHILOSOPHERS

1. "When I consider the short duration of my life, swallowed up in the eternity before and after, the little space which I fill, and even can see, engulfed in the infinite immensity of spaces of which I am ignorant, and which know me not, I am frightened, and am astonished at being here rather than there; for there is no reason why here rather than there, why now rather than then. Who has put me here? By whose order and direction have this place and time been allotted to me?...The eternal silence of these infinite spaces frightens me."
PASCAL, BLAISE. *Pensées.* Trans. W. F. Trotter. New York: E. P. Dutton & Co., 1958.

2. "One day, or one night, a demon will wake you and say to you: this life, as you now live it and have lived it, well, you will have to live it once more, in all its details, even the most minuscule;

every joy, every sorrow…every thought and every sigh…in the same succession, from beginning to end. The same inescapable sequence! And then you will have to start over, again and again… Indefinitely!"
Paraphrase of: NIETZSCHE, FRIEDRICH. *The Gay Science.* Trans. Walter Kaufmann. New York: Vintage, 1974.

3. "The last act is bloody, however pleasant all the rest of the play is: a little earth is thrown at last upon our head, and that is the end forever."
BLAISE, PASCAL. *Pensées.* Trans. John Warrington, ed. Louis Lafuma and H.T. Barnwell. London: J.M. Dent & Sons, 1931.

4. "What is life? An illusion, a shadow, a fiction… All of life is nothing but a dream, and dreams are nothing but dreams."
CALDERÓN DEL LA BARCA, PEDRO. *La vida es sueño.* Madrid: Ediciones Catédra, 2004.
Emma Ramadan's translation of Fouad Laroui's French.

5. "I cannot fear death for as long as I am here, it is not here. And when it will be here, I will no longer be here. Thus, I will never meet death. Thus, I do not need to be afraid of it…"
Paraphrase of: "Death, therefore, the most awful of evils, is nothing to us, seeing that, when we are, death is not come, and, when death is come, we are not."
EPICURUS, *Letter to Menoeceus.* Trans. R. D. Hicks. New York: Charles Scribner's Sons, 1910.
Emma Ramadan's translation of Fouad Laroui's French.

6. "Don't aspire, oh my soul, to immortal life. But exhaust the field of the possible."
PINDAR, *Pythian III.*
Emma Ramadan's translation of Fouad Laroui's French.

7. "The day is rising, we must try to live!"
Paraphrase of: VALÉRY, PAUL. "Le Cimetière marin." *Le Cimetière marin et autres poèmes.* Paris: Larousse, 2016.
Emma Ramadan's translation of Fouad Laroui's French.

8. "One must imagine Sisyphus happy."
CAMUS, ALBERT. *The Myth of Sisyphus and Other Essays.* Trans. Justin O'Brien. New York: Vintage, 1942.

9. "We who perhaps one day shall die, proclaim man as immortal at the flaming heart of the instant."
PERSE, SAINT-JOHN. *Selected Poems.* Ed. Mary Ann Caws. New York: New Directions, 1982.

10. "The whole world are actors."
"Quod fere totus mundus exerceat histrionem."
Commonly attributed to: PETRONIUS. *Policraticus.*

11. "…*d'en soi et de pour soi*, being-in-itself and being-for-itself."
SARTRE, JEAN-PAUL. *Being and Nothingness.* Trans. Hazel E. Barnes. New York: Washington Square Press, 1993.

FOUAD LAROUI was born in 1958 in Oujda, Morocco. After his studies in the Lycée Lyautey (Casablanca), he joined the prestigious École Nationale des Ponts et Chaussées (Paris), where he studied engineering. After having worked in the Office Cherifien des Phosphates company in Khouribga (Morocco), he moved to the United Kingdom where he received a PhD in Economics, and moved to the Netherlands where he currently teaches econometrics and environmental science at the University of Amsterdam. In addition, he is devoted to writing: fiction in French, poetry in Dutch, academic and nonfiction work in English. He has published over twenty novels and collections of short stories, poetry, and essays, and is a literary chronicler for the weekly magazine *Jeune Afrique* and *Economia Magazine*, and the French-Moroccan radio Médi1. *The Curious Case of Doussakine's Trousers* won Laroui his first Prix Goncourt for the short story. Deep Vellum will publish his most recent, Grand Prix Jean Giorno-winning novel *The Tribulations of the Last Sjilmassi*—his first in English—in 2017.

EMMA RAMADAN is a graduate of Brown University, received her Master's in Cultural Translation from the American University of Paris, and recently completed a Fulbright Fellowship for literary translation in Morocco. Her translation of Anne Garréta's *Sphinx* was published by Deep Vellum in spring 2015 and was nominated for the PEN Translation Prize and the Best Translated Book Award. Her translation of Anne Parian's prose poem Monospace was released by La Presse in fall 2015, and her translations of Anne Garréta's Prix Medicis-winning novel *Not One Day*, Fouad Laroui's *The Tribulations of the Last Sjilmassi*, and Brice Matthiuessent's *Revenge of the Translator* will all be published by Deep Vellum in 2017.

Thank you all
for your support.
We do this for you,
and could not do
it without you.

DEEP
VELLUM

DEAR READERS,

Deep Vellum Publishing is a 501c3 nonprofit literary arts organization founded in 2013 with the threefold mission to publish international literature in English translation; to foster the art and craft of translation; and to build a more vibrant book culture in Dallas and beyond. We seek out literary works of lasting cultural value that both build bridges with foreign cultures and expand our understanding of what literature is and what meaningful impact literature can have in our lives.

Operating as a nonprofit means that we rely on the generosity of tax-deductible donations from individual donors, cultural organizations, government institutions, and foundations to provide a of our operational budget in addition to book sales. Deep Vellum offers multiple donor levels, including the LIGA DE ORO and the LIGA DEL SIGLO. The generosity of donors at every level allows us to pursue an ambitious growth strategy to connect readers with the best works of literature and increase our understanding of the world. Donors at various levels receive customized benefits for their donations, including books and Deep Vellum merchandise, invitations to special events, and named recognition in each book and on our website.

We also rely on subscriptions from readers like you to provide an invaluable ongoing investment in Deep Vellum that demonstrates a commitment to our editorial vision and mission. Subscribers are the bedrock of our support as we grow the readership for these amazing works of literature from every corner of the world. The more subscribers we have, the more we can demonstrate to potential donors and bookstores alike the diverse support we receive and how we use it to grow our mission in ever-new, ever-innovative ways.

From our offices and event space in the historic cultural district of Deep Ellum in central Dallas, we organize and host literary programming such as author readings, translator workshops, creative writing classes, spoken word performances, and interdisciplinary arts events for writers, translators, and artists from across the world. Our goal is to enrich and connect the world through the power of the written and spoken word, and we have been recognized for our efforts by being named one of the "Five Small Presses Changing the Face of the Industry" by Flavorwire and honored as Dallas's Best Publisher by *D Magazine*.

If you would like to get involved with Deep Vellum as a donor, subscriber, or volunteer, please contact us at deepvellum.org. We would love to hear from you.

Thank you all. Enjoy reading.

Will Evans
Founder & Publisher
Deep Vellum Publishing

LIGA DE ORO ($5,000+)

Anonymous (2)

LIGA DEL SIGLO ($1,000+)

Allred Capital Management
Ben & Sharon Fountain
Judy Pollock
Life in Deep Ellum
Loretta Siciliano
Lori Feathers
Mary Ann Thompson-Frenk
   & Joshua Frenk
Matthew Rittmayer
Meriwether Evans
Pixel and Texel
Nick Storch
Social Venture Partners Dallas
Stephen Bullock

DONORS

Adam Rekerdres
Alan Shockley
Amrit Dhir
Anonymous
Andrew Yorke
Anthony Messenger
Bob Appel
Bob & Katherine Penn
Brandon Childress
Brandon Kennedy
Caroline Casey
Charles Dee Mitchell
Charley Mitcherson
Cheryl Thompson
Christie Tull
Daniel J. Hale

Ed Nawotka
Rev. Elizabeth
   & Neil Moseley
Ester & Matt Harrison
Grace Kenney
Greg McConeghy
Jeff Waxman
JJ Italiano
Justin Childress
Kay Cattarulla
Kelly Falconer
Linda Nell Evans
Lissa Dunlay
Marian Schwartz
   & Reid Minot
Mark Haber

Mary Cline
Maynard Thomson
Michael Reklis
Mike Kaminsky
Mokhtar Ramadan
Nikki & Dennis Gibson
Olga Kislova
Patrick Kukucka
Richard Meyer
Steve Bullock
Suejean Kim
Susan Carp
Susan Ernst
Theater Jones
Tim Perttula
Tony Thomson

SUBSCRIBERS

Adrian Mitchell
Aimee Kramer
Alan Shockley
Albert Alexander
Aldo Sanchez
Amber Appel
Amrit Dhir
Anandi Rao
Andrea Passwater
Anonymous
Antonia Lloyd-Jones
Ashley Coursey Bull
Barbara Graettinger
Ben Fountain
Ben Nichols
Bill Fisher
Bob Appel
Bradford Pearson
Carol Cheshire
Caroline West
Charles Dee Mitchell
Cheryl Thompson
Chris Fischbach
Chris Sweet
Clair Tzeng
Cody Ross
Colin Winnette
Colleen Dunkel
Cory Howard
Courtney Marie
Courtney Sheedy
David Christensen
David Griffin
David Weinberger
Ed Tallent

Elizabeth Caplice
Erin Kubatzky
Frank Merlino
Greg McConeghy
Horatiu Matei
Ines ter Horst
James Tierney
Jay Geller
Jeanie Mortensen
Jeanne Milazzo
Jennifer Marquart
Jeremy Hughes
Jill Kelly
Joe Milazzo
Joel Garza
John Schmerein
John Winkelman
Jonathan Hope
Joshua Edwin
Julia Rigsby
Julie Janicke Muhsmann
Justin Childress
Kaleigh Emerson
Ken Bruce
Kenneth McClain
Kimberly Alexander
Lea Courington
Lara Smith
Lissa Dunlay
Lori Feathers
Lucy Moffatt
Lytton Smith
Marcia Lynx Qualey
Margaret Terwey

Mies de Vries
Mark Shockley
Martha Gifford
Mary Costello
Matt Bull
Maynard Thomson
Meaghan Corwin
Michael Elliott
Michael Holtmann
Mike Kaminsky
Naomi Firestone-Teeter
Neal Chuang
Nhan Ho
Nick Oxford
Nikki Gibson
Owen Rowe
Patrick Brown
Peter McCambridge
Rainer Schulte
Rebecca Ramos
Richard Thurston
Scot Roberts
Shelby Vincent
Steven Kornajcik
Steven Norton
Susan Ernst
Tara Cheesman-Olmsted
Theater Jones
Tim Kindseth
Todd Jailer
Todd Mostrog
Tom Bowden
Walter Paulson
Will Pepple